Big Sky

Country

www.barbarianspy.com

BarbarianSpy
Toronto, Australia

Big Sky Country

Dirk Hessian

Table of Contents

Chapter One: Altaring Life

Gabe—Gabriel Fortier—could see part way up the center aisle when he turned his head to the left. The altar in the center of the platform at the front of the Duson Christian Church sanctuary was just a table and Gabe was laid out on the dais behind it. The table was covered by an altar cloth, but that didn't go all the way to the floor. The young, dark haired and dusky complexioned man of French Creole extraction, who probably had some Caribbean black in him but far enough in the past only to bring dark and handsome to mind when he was described, was lying on his back on the floor behind the altar in the Evangelical church on the edge of Duson, Louisiana, a few clicks west of Lafayette, Louisiana, just off the highway from New Orleans heading into Texas.

The other man's reddish-brown hair was moving in waves as his head bobbed up and down on Gabe's cock. He'd pulled Gabe's jeans and briefs off and raised the young man's T-shirt over his head, leaving him naked as he was stretched out on the wood floor in the chancel area of the small, weather-beaten chapel. Gabe's legs were spread and bent to give the man room to lie between them. The man was gripping Gabe's hands with his, trapping Gabe under him and controlling him.

Gabe liked to be controlled; it took any sense of guilt for being involved in this away from him—in his mind. He was a complete submissive. He had tried to demure from the act and had struggled a bit when the man had first embraced him, kissed him, and taken him to the floor behind the altar. But once under the man's control, Gabe had gone docile and opened his legs to the man's desire. At that point it became Gabe's desire as well. He was moving his hips now, rhythmically, to move his cock in the man's mouth, going with rather than fighting against the suck, both of them moaning their pleasure.

This wasn't the first time he'd played this game with the man—this game of giving himself as a sacrifice to the man. The first time he'd fucked Gabe in this room, he'd done it up there right on top of the altar. He'd pushed the brass candle sticks and cross right down onto the floor and hoisted Gabe up, already stripped down to naked, and laid him on his back on the altar, with his ass on the edge of one of the narrow sides. Gabe had already been subdued, kissed and fondled, face fucked and finger fucked in the ass, and he was completely subdued, begging for it like he'd gotten it before in the church kitchen and in the man's car.

"Put your ankles on my shoulders," the man had commanded, and Gabe had done that. And then the man mumbled something about sacrifice of the lamb and said, "Stretch your arms straight out, like a crucifix. Sacrifice to me." And Gabe had done that. His elbows had gone to the edge of the altar, front and back, straight out from his side, and his forearms projected over the edges. Then the man put his dick inside Gabe, grabbed him by the waist with both hands, pulled him on and off his cock, and fucked him good. Once the man had gotten his dick inside him, Gabe just lay there, moaning quietly, his face turned toward the empty pews, his pelvis rolled up to accept the man as deep as he could get, and let the man take what he wanted.

This was predominantly a Catholic area, so the congregation of the Evangelical church was small. Gabe's mother had told him there would be no good to be had in going to work part time for "those Evangelical nuts" his last semester of high school over in Lafayette, where Gabe had been a standout on the baseball team. If she could see him now, the older man lying between Gabe's thighs, his arms wrapped around Gabe's legs and his hands gripping Gabe's hands to hold him trapped in place, his mouth sucking on Gabe's cock, and Gabe moving his hips in rhythm with the suck, she'd be livid. She'd be petrified.

She'd probably be dead, Gabe thought. She'd have a coronary. She'd also read him the riot act about being just like his father, who had left her high and dry, running off with a younger man, having come back from the Second World War in Europe eight years earlier with a nervous tick and more interest in men than women. But Gabe had seen how happy his father had been with his young man and he'd not taken the insult like his mother had. It had actually helped him consider possibilities and examine his desire structure. That had led him to be on the floor here, behind the altar. This wasn't his first time with the charismatic older man, Elijah Parker, either. It wasn't the first time the man had gotten his dick inside Gabe.

Gabe murmured resistance and struggled a bit each time, but he was happy enough when he at least symbolically came under the man's control and was moved into the suck and fuck.

Gabe gasped and arched his back as a wet finger entered his ass and pressed in. His control established, Elijah loosened his grip on Gabe's legs and freed the young man's hands. Gabe bent his legs more, placing his bare feet flat on the dusty boards of the floor behind the altar, and widened his stance. His hands went to the back of Elijah's head, his fingers digging into the wavy reddish-brown hair, holding the man's head close in for his deep-throating possession of Gabe's young cock. He moaned as Elijah, grasping and separating his buttocks and now, with fingers of both hands inside his channel, went into overdrive in his mouth action on Gabe's cock.

9

The younger man knew that Elijah would want him to come in the man's throat and then he'd cover Gabe and fuck him. That had been the liberation Elijah Parker had brought to Gabe—he'd taken Gabe from not knowing and aching to try it to having done it and learned that ecstasy was having a man inside you. In contrast to Gabe's nakedness, the man was still dressed, in black. Only his fly was unzipped and his dick, in upcurved erection, was exposed.

He desperately wanted Gabe—a man like Elijah had to fully possess a young man like Gabe. He had to merge with the young man, be one with him, dominate him completely. This uncontrollable desire for him drove Gabe's arousal as well and his willingness to lie under the man. No one had wanted Gabe the way Elijah did.

With a groan and a gasp, Gabe came in Elijah's throat and, knowing that the older man would want to go immediately into the fuck, raised his legs, folding his legs up into his chest and tucking his knees into the hollow of his shoulders, rolling his pelvis up, as the older man moved up on his body. Elijah, now hovering over Gabe and looking down into the younger man's face, capturing his focus, their eyes locked, and exercising the charismatic control over Gabe that had the young man under his sexual control, placed the heel of his left hand down on the wooden floor beside Gabe's right ear and positioned the bulb of his cock at Gabe's entrance. With a grunt from Elijah and a gasp from Gabe, Elijah was in to the depth of the bulb. His right hand came down beside Gabe's left ear and the older man was hovering over Gabe's torso, staring down into the young man's face, observing every expression on it.

He saw the grimace in the young man's face and felt the palms of Gabe's hands slide under his waistband and cup his buttocks. He then felt the pressure of Gabe pulling his pelvis forward and heard the whispered, "Now. Do it.

10

Fuck me," as the pressure from the young man's hands caused him to gain a few inches. Gabe was panting. Then Gabe was giving a little cry, arching his back more and projecting his pain-pleasure in his eyes and yawning mouth as Elijah slid inside him. He was filling, stretching Gabe's channel walls and moving deep inside him, possessing Gabe in the most intimate way possible. The pumping started immediately, with Gabe's hands going to Elijah's shoulders and his own pelvis going into motion, moving with Elijah's thrusts.

They were merged, one again, Elijahgabe, moving as one, perfect, divine machine.

When the rhythm had been established, Gabe relaxed his body and let his arms stretch out straight from his sides in the cruciform pattern he knew Elijah liked him to be in when they fucked to symbolize his total submission, their oneness. The young man let his head loll off to the left side, his eyes focused on the triangular perspective of the center aisle of the congregation hall running from the raised platform the altar was on back toward the door at the back of the hall.

He concentrated on the cock moving inside him. It was neither particularly thick nor long, but this was Gabe's first anal-sex man, so he'd taken no other man inside him and had nothing to compare Elijah against. All he knew was that he felt wanted and fully possessed. He found it filling and masterful. He also, strangely enough, felt a sense of power and control of his own—the sense of victory and accomplishment that a man like Elijah Parker wanted to be inside him—was willing to take the risks of fucking him, barely legal, in the chancel, behind the altar.

He sighed, straining his pelvis up, into Elijah's groin, as he felt the older man tense, jerk, and ejaculate inside his channel. Gabe's eyes had been closed, but, as Elijah went through a series of after thrusts inside Gabe before

11

withdrawing, and gave Gabe a low sob that let Gabe know how much of this was his own control, Gabe opened his eyes, looking out under the altar toward the pews in the hall.

He froze as he saw, just on the other side of the altar, the black Mary Jane shoes.

"Pastor Elijah Parker," the angry, despairing voice of a woman cut through the silence in the hall. "You said never again. You promised."

The beginning of the wrath of Mrs. Elijah Parker, wife of the pastor of the Duson Christian Church.

Chapter Two: Beautiful Downtown Guthrie

He'd opened Adrian's letter so often that now, as he read it under the nightlight in the bus driving west from Duson, it developed a split along the fold line through the middle. He'd had the letter for four months and had opened it several times a day. He'd almost sent a response, but then Pastor Parker had cornered him one day and maneuvered him to lay down and open his legs to him and Gabe had been distracted from Adrian's proposal. The pastor's wife, silent before but not this time, had caused Gabe's attention to be focused back on Adrian as the best means of escape.

Adrian had been older than he was—two years older. They'd been in high school in Lafayette together and on the baseball team together. Gabe had lived with Adrian's family for the years of high school, his mother arranging for him to be at a better school than the one in Duson, a school that had a baseball team. She also wanted him out of the house and, she thought, safe from a man who had come home from the war in Europe having developed a desire for younger men.

That hadn't worked out exactly as she had wanted it to.

Adrian had known what he wanted before he'd left high school for Texas Tech, in Lubbock, on a sports scholarship there. His parents wanted him to study to be an engineer but Adrian wanted to trade on his looks and charisma and be a movie star. What Adrian had really wanted—and had easily been able to get—was men. He'd had one the summer before going to college—an ex-soldier friend of Gabe's father. Adrian liked to both give and take. There might even have been something with Gabe's father after his father had unexpectedly visited Gabe in Lafayette, but Adrian never would confirm that. And there had been a couple of "almost" times with Gabe himself, although Adrian had always said they needed to wait until Gabe was older to do it all. Fondling and some shared masturbation wasn't "it all."

Gabe was older now, and he had this letter from Adrian, urging him to come out to Lubbock and live with Adrian. There were schools Gabe could go to there. He might even be able to get into the athletic program at Texas Tech, like Adrian had. Or he could get a job. He could live with Adrian. Adrian hadn't been able to forget Gabe, he said in the letter. He wanted Gabe to come out to Lubbock and give it a try.

It hadn't seemed like a possible option before, but now it looked like the only option. At least it was worth a try, if Adrian hadn't forgotten him in the four months since he'd sent the offer. If nothing else, if Gabe could get to Lubbock, Adrian would put him up until he could find something to do. He couldn't stay in Duson. Mrs. Parker had made it quite clear he couldn't stay, calling him Satan's spawn, blaming what had happened with the pastor on him, saying he was temptation and temptation had to be rooted out—that the minister was a good man being tempted and needed help to fight the temptation. His mother had agreed with the part of it being his fault, but she said it was because he'd mixed with godless Evangelicals—he'd turned his back on the Catholic Church. He was too much like his father—more like his father than his mother wanted to talk about.

All in all, everyone in Duson was happy to be rid of him. They weren't happy enough to raise sufficient funds to get him all the way to Lubbock on the bus, though. Everyone, Evangelicals and Catholics alike, had said that faith would get him there and all they had to do was to get him started there—to get him far enough out of Duson that it would be better to keep going than trying to come back.

He knew he had to make money along the way. That's why, when the bus made a rest stop in Godknowswhere south of Shreveport at 3:00 in the morning, Gabe went behind the bathrooms with another guy. The guy had talked Gabe up and showed signs of wanting to feel him up at the last rest stop they'd been at. This time, he walked by Gabe in the aisle of the bus, gave him a meaningful look, and showed him a folded five-dollar bill. Gabe, needing a five pretty bad, rose from his seat with a sigh and followed the man out of the bus. He was a tall, gaunt man, with greasy black hair that flopped down in his craggy face. He probably wasn't over thirty-five, but he'd obviously led a hard life. Well, he couldn't exactly be a Rockefeller if he was on a bus going cross country through Louisiana into Texas. He maybe was from Texas and going home, because he was wearing worn slim-line jeans, with a plaid shirt above and scruffy cowboy boots below—the uniform of the Texas working class in the mid 1950s.

Gabe got out of the bus in time to see the man walk back toward the bathrooms accessed off the side of the combined gas station and diner and then drift past those doors and around the back of the building in the shadows and between the bushes and the gas station wall.

When Gabe got around the corner of the building, the man was leaning his back into the cinderblock rear wall of the building in the dim light filtering around there from a bulb on the wall outside the doors to the bathrooms. His pelvis was jutting forward, he had his shirt unbuttoned and flared, showing a thinnish but muscle-hard chest, covered with tattoos. He already had his fly unzipped, his jeans flared open, and his dick out. He was fisting his cock with one hand and holding the five spot in the other. As Gabe went down on his knees in front of the man, the money was shoved under the neck opening of his T-shirt with one hand and the guy's other hand was guiding the young man's mouth to his cock.

As he went down, Gabe saw that one of the tattoos on the man's torso, one above and to the right of the curve of his belly, gave the words 175th Infantry, with crossed rifles under it. So, he was probably one of those soldiers coming back from World War Two and not being able to totally settle down to a domestic life. Gabe got the idea that the man, like his father, must have acquired the habit of going with men during the war and still held it in his memory, because, while Gabe was sucking him off, the man held one of Gabe's hands to the tattoo and gave a few deep sighs. That didn't keep him from holding Gabe's face to his crotch until Gabe was gagging on the hard cock before letting him come up for air briefly.

Time was short but the man was worked up, so Gabe had taken the guy's cum on his cheek in under ten minutes of sucking and stroking.

As they got back on the bus, the man guided Gabe down the aisle with his hand and indicated that he wanted Gabe to come back to the back of the bus with him. Gabe acted like he didn't get the hint, though, and smoothly turned into his seat and turned his head to the window. There were fewer than a half dozen people on the Greyhound bus and they all settled in for the night soon after the driver pulled away from the stop in Godknowswhere. All the lights were off in the bus, and the sounds of light snores were all that could be heard. Gabe

16

woke to his shoulder being shaken and he looked up to see the cowboy leaning over him from the aisle, smiling and holding another five-dollar bill. He gestured toward the back of the bus.

On the very back row of seats, Gabe and the man sat close together, and Gabe earned the second five dollars by bending over in the seat, the man holding the young man's hand to his military tattoo with his shirt unbuttoned, and Gabe sucking the man off again. This was followed by Gabe lying back in the seat while the man did him with a hand job, lowering his face to take Gabe's cum in his mouth when he came. Gabe returned to his seat and slept through past Shreveport. The guy he'd serviced must have gotten off there, because he no longer was on the bus when Gabe woke. It was a relief to Gabe to know the stranger was gone and wouldn't be giving Gabe knowing looks or hitting on him again, even if he had money to pay for it.

It was only ten dollars, but that was pretty good money in 1953 and Gabe figured it would get him fifty miles closer to Lubbock than the money he'd been given in Duson to get the devil out of town would do. He also figured he was going to have to suck off some more toads between here and there if he wanted to get to Lubbock at all. He thought he probably was lucky there were men who had acquired a preference for other men while they were in the war. That's where Pastor Parker told Gabe he'd acquired that sin, or, as he liked to call it, the temptation of Satan. Of course he'd usually been busy fucking Gabe when he'd been mouthing off about sin and damnation. He'd even called Gabe Satan a time or two while he was pounding Gabe's ass.

* * * *

17

"Here we are," the bus driver called out. He pulled the bus over in front of a gas station at the beginning of a one-main-street town, with just one line of houses on streets on either side of the one with storefronts on it.

"We're where?" a woman near the front of the bus asked in a weary voice. "Didn't we just stop for breakfast and a coffee less than an hour ago?"

"You, son, in the white T-shirt. I'm talking to you." The bus driver was turned in his seat, looking back into the interior of the bus, beyond the woman whose question he was ignoring.

"Me?" Gabe asked, turning his face to the front of the bus. He'd been daydreaming, reviewing his life up to this point and not finding that much to be impressed by. Good thing he was good-looking and willing to lay down for a guy. A lot of guys had come back from the war with that itch. Adrian told him there were men in Lubbock who'd be willing to give him a start if he gave them something. By his reckoning they should be hitting Lubbock any time now.

"Yes, you. This is where your ticket takes you, son. You're home."

"Home?" Gabe said, looking around. This didn't look like anyone's home really—at least anyone not trapped here: two blocks of storefronts at a cross-road of two minor highways, with a row of houses all looking alike on either side and then nothing but flat semidesert land in all directions.

"Take a look at your ticket. My clipboard here says you bought a ticket to Guthrie."

"I'm going to Lubbock," Gabe said, scrounging around for his bus ticket. "Well, shit," he then said. The ticket, indeed, was for Guthrie, Texas. He'd had a bit of a wrangle with the station master selling tickets back at the Lafayette Greyhound bus station. He'd tried to tell Gabe

18

that the fare to Lubbock was more than Gabe saw marked on the sign. They'd argued for nearly a minute, with the line building behind Gabe, and the ticket seller had finally given up and issued a ticket. Gabe could understand now that the ticket seller hadn't lost—he just gave Gabe a ticket for how far he thought the fare give would cover regardless of what the sign said.

"You can go to Lubbock for another fifteen dollars," the bus driver said. "Lubbock is about eighty miles further west down this road. Or you can get out in Guthrie. Sorry, Them's your choices."

All Gabe had left was the ten dollars the guy had given him for sex the previous night back before Shreveport.

"Well shit," Gabe said again.

He stood by the side of the road, his duffle bag on the ground next to him, and coughed, as the bus covered him in a cloud of dust and exhaust fumes as it pulled back onto the road. He watched it drive through the business section of Guthrie, and he was still watching it over five minutes later, disappearing into the flat, arid ranch land of central northern Texas. Then heaving his duffle on his back and holding its strap with a fist at his right shoulder, he turned and walked into Guthrie.

It took him fifteen minutes to come out at the other end of the town—and that was while looking in every storefront, not just to see what stores and businesses were there but to check for "help wanted" signs. He was a realist. He figured if he was going to scrape up enough money to make it that last eighty miles into Lubbock, it was going to be because he did some work for someone to get the fare. He figured that he could cover the two residential streets of the town in twenty minutes or so. He'd done some construction and grass cutting work—not that much grass was growing in this town. If there weren't any signs out on the businesses, he'd look for a house that needed work he thought he could do.

The only "help wanted" sign he saw as he walked to the western end of town, which ended in a rail head and stock pens, was in the window of a diner that had a "Lone Star Diner" sign over the door. The sign here was a bit cryptic: "Young man wanted to serve and for man sport. Room, Board, Tips." Not being able to figure out fully what that meant, he kept on walking, coming up with no other prospects as he hit the edge of town. He walked back, stopping at the diner, taking a deep breath, and entered. As he entered, he turned and picked up the sign that was in the window.

Just walking into the diner made the scene inside freeze and six sets of eyes focus on Gabe, all of them taking on a speculative look. The biggest—as in heaviest—guy was standing behind a lunch counter and leaning into it. He had a toothpick in what was sort of a doughy face under a bald head with a salt-and-pepper fringe of hair. He wore a white apron, splotched with spots of "you don't want to know," hanging over a white T-shirt with the arms rolled up, showing bulging biceps, and a packet of Lucky Strikes hung up above the left bicep. The guy took in that Gabe had picked the "help wanted" sign out of the window and then his eyes took a slow, ground up assessment of Gabe.

A young woman was coming through a door to the kitchen with two plates in her hand as Gabe entered the diner. She too stopped dead in her tracks and gave him the once over—also not missing that he was holding the "help wanted" sign. She was short and thin, with blonde, very likely peroxided, hair, a face that was overly made up, and tightly clothed in jeans and a revealing pull-over blouse, all of which loudly expressed "tired but available for not much of a fee."

The other four sets of eyes belonged to diner patrons—three cowboy types at the table where the waitress was headed with the plates, and to which she resumed her progress after the short pause to take Gabe in, and another guy alone at a table, who was dressed similarly to the three cowboys but who was older—in his late thirties, at least—and who seemed more in the class of rancher than cowpoke. Their food starting to arrive, the cowboys readjusted the focus of their attention to food. The lone diner continued to watch Gabe with interest.

"This sign, advertising for help," Gabe said, looking at the bruiser behind the bar, who obviously represented management here.

"You interested?" The man asked. His voice was deep and rough. His attention had gone to the duffel bag Gabe had slung on his back.

"Might be, if I can figure out what help is needed," Gabe said.

"Well, son, why don't you step back to my office and I'll explain it to you." The bruiser came out from behind the counter and moved to a booth at the back corner of the diner. The table had stacks of paper on it, indicating that it probably *was* the guy's office. "Two coffees when you get a chance, Carol," he flipped in the direction of the waitress as he guided Gabe to the booth with a hand on the small of his back.

The touch was unnecessary, and Gabe got the impression that the man had put his hand there on purpose—like to get Gabe's reaction. The young man immediately thought there might be a sexual interest there, as Pastor Elijah had done the same thing months earlier and Gabe hadn't shied away, which had led to so much more than just a touch on the back.

Gabe didn't shrink away from this man's touch any more than he had Pastor Elijah's. Compared to the pastor,

21

this guy was a toad, but he also had control over the only job prospect Gabe could see in this town—which was the only evidence of civilization for miles that Gabe could pick out in any direction as he walked the town's one business street. And maybe, if he was interested in pay for a lay in the hay rather than giving Gabe a job, Gabe could scrape enough together to resume his trip to Lubbock. Besides, Gabe was interested in what men did to him. He liked to be fucked.

The blowsy blonde waitress, who Gabe gathered was named Carol, interrupted her service to the cowboys to rustle up coffees for the manager and Gabe. This didn't raise an objection from the third cowboy, who didn't have his meal yet, so Gabe got the idea that the restaurant guy had a "do not mess with me" persona that was generally recognized and respected in this town. That was good to know. If he had to, he'd go all submissive to get this job long enough to put together the ongoing bus fare to Lubbock.

"You're not from here, are you?" the man said when they were settled in the booth.

"No, Sir, I'm from Louisiana, passing through to Lubbock, and short on means to get there," Gabe answered. He thought it best to be up front about it. If the guy was looking for a permanent waiter, he wasn't going to want to hire Gabe. "Does the bus to Lubbock even stop here, though?"

"When we ask it to. New Orleans, you say?" the man asked.

"Lafayette," Gabe answered. "A bit closer to here than New Orleans—and a lot smaller and duller."

"You're dark, but not nigger looking—"

"I'm Creole," Gabe answered. "It's sort of a common Louisiana trait." If he could, he'd fend off questions of race and proportion of blood, while not lying

22

about it. He got the impression that being black wasn't going to cut it here. There was very little black in him—no different than nearly every other person native to Louisiana—but with the 1-percent rule—proportion of racial origin in your makeup that was black—that was starting to get a lot of attention in the States in the mid 1950s, he was a bit behind the eight ball on this.

"Ah, Creole," the man said, obviously thinking this made a difference without really know what Creole meant. Gabe took it as a sign that the man was interested. "That's OK. On you it looks good. You're a good-looking kid. Probably would be good for business."

Yes, the guy seemed to be interested, Gabe thought. He wondered if he should give a signal of some sort that he could be had, if that was what was on the man's mind. "My name is Gabe. Gabe's short for Gabriel. Gabriel Fortier. I'd do pretty much anything a boss wanted me to do. Anything." He sort of fluttered his eyelashes at the man. They were long and curly.

"Funny name. Sounds French." He didn't seem to have caught the meaning of how cooperative Gabe could be.

"It is," Gabe said. "Louisiana was settled by the French and the Spanish. It's a Creole name." He almost pushed his leg forward to make contact with the man's leg under the booth table, but he still wasn't sure enough for that. He'd signaled and hadn't received a telling response. He knew he wasn't good with this. Adrian and the pastor— and a couple of other men who would remain nameless— had seduced him, and he'd been pretty dumb about what they wanted for an embarrassingly long time. Sometimes they could get their dick in him before he knew he was being fucked.

"Ah, a Creole name." It came out like he still didn't know what the word had to do with anything, other than it claimed the young guy wasn't black.

"I'm Sam Waller. I own this dump. And you say you're looking for a job, but just drifting through? The drifting through part is OK; just about everyone here is drifting through. Even the houses you see here are temporary housing. Two big ranches around here own most of the town, including all of those houses. The 6666—four sixes—Ranch and the Pitchfork Ranch. Both have been here for over a hundred years; Guthrie wouldn't be here at all if they hadn't been here. They don't own this diner, but this diner wouldn't be here without those two ranches. Are you following what I'm saying, Gabe? I take it you want me to call you Gabe, not Gabriel. Gabe sounds solid; Gabriel sounds . . . well, not solid. This isn't a fancy town."

"Yes, Gabe is fine. And I think I follow. These two ranches are what keeps this town open and when they say 'jump,' everyone here says 'how high?'" Taking a chance, Gabe moved his leg forward and rubbed it up against Sam's. He was careful to put it on the outer side of the man's leg. Inner side was a declaration of top; outer declaration of bottom, his memory of what Adrian had told him coming into play. In either case, he could claim he thought it was a table leg if it didn't have the desired effect. He also laid his forearm on the table, in case Sam wanted to put his hand on it. Sam did want to do that, and Gabe gave a little shudder, which he remembered from what Adrian had told him, and looked into the man's eyes. The man also didn't remark on Gabe's leg rubbing his.

Gabe didn't see what he had been told to expect to see in Sam's eyes, though. There was no interest or lust to be seen there.

"That's right," Sam said. "And, since the war, some men who have come to work on those ranches have had different interests and needs than generations before them. And it's getting harder to find men willing to take on the cowboy life now. Those two big ranches are interested in keeping their men happy—all of them, even ones with peculiar interests, as long as they do a good day's work and don't keep other cowboys from doing theirs. Which leads us to that 'help wanted' sign you have in your hand. You're wondering what that 'and for man sport' business is about, aren't you?"

"Yeah, I guess so. The rest of it is for a waiter's job, I guess."

"You got that right. But there's more to the job than that—like there's more to Carol's job—the waitress over there—than just slinging plates. A diner in a town this small has to do what it has to do to stay open. Jobs here have to do double duty and they have to meet the needs that are going in town. You understand that much?"

"Yes, Sir," Gabe answered. He looked down at the hand that was on his forearm and considered his leg up against Sam's under the table. He thought he knew where this was headed—and why it would be part of the job—but the man wasn't putting out the signals like Adrian said a man interested would do.

By now, a man interested in fucking him should be doing something more with his legs under the table. As Pastor Elijah had demonstrated when they'd been alone in the church kitchen for lunch, he could be expected to have both of his legs somehow between Gabe's under the table top, and pressing Gabe's thighs open with his knees. And he should be doing stuff with his fingers on Gabe's forearm—playing with the hair there or something. And the looks he was giving Gabe should be undressing looks. But Gabe wasn't getting anything like that from Sam, even though there was touching.

"I think you understand what the 'man sport' part of the sign is, Gabe. There are two types of men sniffing around for it in this town. Most are sniffing for woman, women like Carol. Some, though, are sniffing for male tail. I think I'm right that you're homo—that you'll let a man fuck you and you'll will take money for it. Am I wrong? If I'm wrong, I apologize, but then this interview is over. That's what 'man sport' means on that sign. It's pretty straightforward really. The diner gives the venue and the connection—and you get a cut of what comes in."

"No, you're not wrong," Gabe said. And to make sure it all was clear. "So, you're saying the job would be both being a waiter in here and letting men fuck me for money in this room the sign says goes with the job."

"Bingo, Gabe," Sam said, with a smile. "I'm glad we didn't have to beat around the bush on this. The two big ranches here are interested in having prostitutes their men can go to when they are in town—and they are having cowboys now who, some of them, want to fuck a man rather than a woman. I think it's a war thing. Our boys went off to the second world war, needed a release for their cum, and didn't always have a woman around. So they did each other, and decided after they came home that they wanted to continue doing each other. So, yes, that's the job. You'd work here in the diner and when there was a man who wanted to pay to fuck you, you'd work in your bedroom upstairs. For the waiter job, you'd get the room, board, and tips. For what you'd get for fucks, you'd get a third of what they pay, and the rest goes to the house. You understand? We good on that?"

There was only a slight pause. Gabe didn't have much of a choice and it wasn't like he wasn't giving sex when he needed to to survive. He was just happy that there would be men who wanted to fuck him for money. Sam

26

went on to cover that, having taken his hand away and moved his leg back.

"That's why it would be OK with me that you were just drifting through. It's not easy to fill this slot, although I have some prospects who might show up in a few weeks or a month. But this is the sort of thing where men paying money like to have variety. And, I gotta say, you're one sexy little piece. I could tell as soon as you walked through the door that you'd be a hit around here in this job. So, the job's yours if you pass the entrance test."

"The entrance test?" Gabe asked. "So, you want me to go upstairs with you and give you sex?"

Sam laughed. It wasn't a pleasant laugh, though. "Shit, no, I'm not queer. I was just testing you to make sure you were. One of the big honchos over at the Brighton Ranch—one nearly as big as the 6666 or Pitchfork—is a power fucker, and I'll let him decide if you're good enough. He likes to get to them when their fresh. I suspect, though, that if you'll take a guy's dick without fainting you'll be good enough. You're certainly the best looker we've had in here since I had to lay a homo on as part of the service. You've taken a big dick before, haven't you?"

"Yes, Sir," Gabe answered. The biggest dick he'd taken was Pastor Parker's and that wasn't much bigger than any other he'd taken. It wasn't as big as Adrian's that Gabe had jacked off with his hand a time or three. But Gabe wanted the jcb, so he'd do whatever size dick showed up until he had the money to get to Lubbock.

The rancher's name was Sterling Fisher. He was a good six foot six, nearly ten inches taller than Gabe, and a hefty 230 pounds, all in well-distributed muscle on the mature frame of an outdoor's man in his late forties. He had a mane of graying hair, a ruggedly handsome face, the cock of a horse, outstanding vigor and virility, and the cruelty of a matinee villain.

Over the space of two and a half hours, he plowed Gabe in several different positions, all dominating ones, and ejaculated twice, bringing cum out of Gabe four times. Gabe had never been taken this fully or roughly before. Fisher pounded him hard and deep, giving no quarter, laughing when, with a groan, Gabe laid himself out in the cruciform position Pastor Elijah had enjoyed so much as a symbol of Gabe's total surrender, and arched his back and put his pelvis into a counterthrust motion, when the rancher slid inside him deep and hovered over his body, doing pushups above him. The bed frame creaked, squealed, and thumped against the wall in the rhythm of the fuck, a sound Gabe would be hearing in stereo on Friday and Saturday nights as Carol was doing the same business that he did in the room next door to his.

Gabe could now answer the question of how the pastor compared to other men—or at least to Sterling Fisher. He in no way compared to this robust rancher in girth, length, or vigor. It had been hard for Gabe to take the cock in the initial fuck—painful, and he didn't open for it as he had for the pastor's. The pastor's cock didn't make the demands on his channel that the rancher's did. Fisher kept growling, "Open, open to me," as if Gabe's channel would know how to accommodate a cock that size. And then, when it was a good five inches inside him, Fisher said, in a more soothing voice, "Relax to me. Take it, take it all," and stopped pressing, just held there as they both panted and he kissed Gabe on the lips and stroked his ass cheeks.

They both felt Gabe relax and open. His channel did, after all, know what to do. Fisher then moved a hand to the small of Gabe's back, pulling him onto the shaft, while his cock glided in for those last few inches. Gabe moaned and sighed as then the pumping started, at first slow and shallow, eventually hard, vigorous, and in long sweeps, with Gabe's pelvis matching the primeval rhythm of the fuck. Gabe's channel had stretched and stretched for the man, almost to splitting, and each time he came—which was twice—it was in a gusher that Gabe could believe was flowing up into his stomach.

Gabe was left, exhausted and moaning, stretched out on the bed in the room on the second floor of the diner, in a completely open, vulnerable stance, which Fisher found so arousing that, after a steak dinner in the diner, he climbed the stairs and did Gabe again. This time Gabe received more pleasure than pain from the fucking. He had been reamed to the rancher's specifications, his channel knew this cock now and blossomed open to it as it sank inside, and he was able to concentrate this time in moving with the man in the rhythm of the fuck.

When the rancher was done and gave his report to Sam, he declared Gabe to be "a really nice piece of ass." "He starts like a virgin and finishes like a whore. He do that for other men and you've got a little goldmine here. I'll be a regular," and, with that, Gabe had a job, a room, and three square meals in the dusty little town of Guthrie, Texas.

~

Chapter Three: The Charmer on the Motorcycle

The same guy—the late-thirties rancher who had been the lone diner at a table—that first day Gabe had some into the Lone Star Diner in search of a job, was coming in three or four times a week by the time Gabe had been a waiter there for three weeks. He and Gabe were on speaking terms. His name was Frank Doyle, he owned a cattle spread called Sunshine north of town that was more than a thousand acres but that ranked as small by the area standards. He said it was at least a forty-five minute drive into Guthrie from his spread and he suggested more than once that Gabe might like to come out and see his ranch.

What was most evident was that he had a crush on Gabe and mooned over him but that he was too reticent to ask for what he wanted. Sam Waller made no bones about what Gabe would do for a customer if he had the money for it—although the man sex business wasn't too brisk, Frank had seen more than one cowboy with his tongue hanging out and a bulge in his jeans go upstairs with Gabe and come back down with a silly grin on his face. And the few times Sterling Fisher came into town to lay Gabe, anyone in the diner could hear the thumping of the bed legs on the floor and headboard against the wall of Gabe's room above the diner. But, although Frank surely had the money as easily if not more easily than the cowboys coming into town off the 6666 and Pitchfork ranches, into Gabe's fourth week at the diner, he hadn't made a move.

Men like Frank wanted more than the sex. Men like him often are looking for companionship and a long-term relationship. Gabe decided that Frank wouldn't make the move unless Gabe signaled he'd give it to him for free— that it was more than just a trick for Gabe. Gabe was, in fact, attracted to Frank, who was all that aroused Gabe, but Sam had made clear there would be no giveaways or the progression on that would never stop. So, Gabe and Frank were friendly with each other in a Mexican standoff sort of way.

That was until the day that Collin Chisholm roared into town.

Gabe was standing by Frank at Frank's table and the rancher had, for the first time, palmed Gabe's ass in a hand while they were talking, which was a bold move for the shy rancher. Frank was quite good looking and he appeared to have a nice body. Gabe found him easy to talk to and attractive. He had a couple of men working his ranch with him, but he put in a full day's work outside himself, so he was lean and muscular and tanned. He dressed clean and neatly, in tight jeans, with a nice bulge in the crotch, and a plaid cotton shirt, cowboy boots and a ten-gallon hat. He seemed to keep his body clean too, and he always smelled nice, not something to take for granted from cowboys in these parts. There were no complaints about him in that department and it was clear to Gabe that the man wanted him. So Gabe was teasing the man along. They'd finally gotten to having established that, yes, Frank was interested, and, yes, he knew there was a price involved, and, no, that didn't deter him. It was like Frank had gotten across that barrier at last.

"I like you just fine, Frank, and I think we'd be good together," Gabe had said, following that with a "maybe you'd like . . ." It was midafternoon, after the diner had cleared of the lunchtime crowd—not that there ever was much of a crowd. Sam and his wife, the cook, were back in the kitchen and cleaning up. Carol was on a smoking break, but she could be called back to watch the front whenever Gabe had someone he needed to take upstairs.

All systems were go for Gabe and Frank to get together at last. Both men obviously wanted it.

But then they heard it, the roar of a motorcycle coming in from the west. It arrested their attention, as this wasn't exactly motorcycle country, and Frank backed off from Gabe. Something strange was happening that demanded everyone's attention. Everything was too far from everything else in the big sky country. Everyone around here moved in pickup trucks. You couldn't have started too far away in terms of Texas distance and be riding a cycle.

But someone was. Someone was riding a motorcycle who pulled up right outside the diner. Not long after the motor was cut, the door to the diner opened, and Mr. Magnificent strutted in.

He was an Adonis—a bit over six feet, movie-star handsome, not more than twenty-five, muscular, sultry and dangerous looking, decked out in black leather, and walking like he owned the place—not just the diner or the town, but the universe. Taking a look around the diner, with his eyes stopping on Gabe and giving him a million-dollar smile, the handsome stranger walked to the lunch counter and mounted a stool like he was seating himself on a horse or his Harley-Davidson, resting outside the diner at the hitching post—or mounting his lover. His legs were spread on the stool as a man would do who had to give his basket plenty of space to fill up. Gabe cut away from Frank and scooted behind the counter in time to be there when Mr. Magnificent settled on his stool.

"What'll you have?" Gabe asked.

"What are you giving?" the young Adonis asked. He had a slow and easy smile, one of possession.

"Would you like to see a menu?" Gabe asked. He spread his arms and placed his hands on the surface of his side of the counter. The Adonis wouldn't know it, and Gabe himself didn't realize it, but he was already taking the cruciform position of total, sacrificial sexual submission that Pastor Parker had trained him to. But, somehow, from the look the young man gave Gabe, the Adonis *did* know it. The seduction was over. The Adonis could have laid Gabe out on the counter there, in front of Frank and the other diners, and fucked him, and Gabe would have submitted to him.

Gabe curled his fingers and set his hand down on the knuckles, touching the tip of his thumb of each hand to the index finger, making an "O" opening. He did it with each hand. It was a signal he'd been told to use to identify upstairs business. He was symbolically offering up the sheath for a man's cock—either mouth or ass, customer's choice. His heart and cock took a lurch when the gorgeous young man spread his arms on the customer side of the counter and inserted his middle fingers in the sheaths Gabe was providing with his hands. He knew the code, and he was a dominant top. The offer and dominant assertion were complete. The rest was just preliminary banter. They both knew where this was going.

"I was told this was the place in town to come to get a man's itch scratched. If I were to look at a menu, would you be on it?"

"You were told—"

"That this was the place to get male tail, yes. Are you the male tail here?"

"If you wanted me to be, I could be—and if you had the money."

"And what if I didn't want to spend the money before getting a sample? Suppose I might be a repeat customer if I liked what I was served the first time?"

"Well, that's not the way it works."

"You serve beer here? Break out a couple and let's talk a few minutes."

They stood there, across from each other, with the counter between them, attached at the fingers of one hand, Collin Chisholm's middle finger rubbing inside the sheath provided by Gabe's hand—having established each other's names—and lifting beers with the other hands. And then a second beer for each of them.

They were leaning in to each other, eventually with their foreheads pressed together and their eyes locked onto each others. Somewhere before the first beers had been finished off, Frank stood, took one last, forlorn look at Gabe, and left the diner.

Collin was whispering to Gabe and Gabe was mesmerized by him.

"You're a real honey. I want to get my dick in you. You'd like that just fine, I guarantee it. But I want you to want it so much that I don't have to pay for it. That cheapens it."

"Well, we couldn't go upstairs," Gabe murmured. "Maybe around back. My boss can't see us, though. Go on out and around the side of the building. I'll meet you there."

When Collin had left, Gabe went to the kitchen door and called for Carol, saying he had to run an errand and could she cover for a while.

The area for the trash cans at the side of the building was walled off. Collin fucked Gabe against the wall next to the trash bins. Gabe was naked. Collin had wanted to touch him everywhere and Gabe had moaned for him and gone hard as he did so. Then Collin had unzipped his black leather jacket and pulled it off his back, revealing a magnificent smooth chest, as Gabe knelt in front of him and made Collin's cock hard with his mouth. Only Collin's cock and balls jutted out of his unzipped and flared black leather pants, as he lifted Gabe up from his knees, growled for Gabe to hook his legs on his hips, entered him, and fucked him hard and deep.

"Wasn't that all you ever could have wanted?" Collin asked after they'd both come.

"Yes." Gabe answered. Then he added, "Yes, yes, yes."

When they came back around the side of the diner and Collin was mounting his motorcycle, Gabe spied Frank Doyle standing across the street in front of a shop and watching them. Gabe's eyes followed Collin riding off to the west of town. The touch on his arm made him turn. Frank was right there, lust and need in his eyes, a wad of bills in his hand. He fucked Gabe to the quick of him with a long, thick dick in a clutch missionary position in Gabe's room above the diner, the two of them working together like long-time lovers and coming together. And then, after a rest, Frank fucked him again, with Gabe on his belly and Frank stretched out on top of him, every square inch of the two that could be in contact caressing each other, and just Frank's pelvis languidly moving, rising and falling, as he fucked Gabe thick and deep. Gabe had fallen into an exhausted sleep when, twilight falling on the town, Frank rose, dressed, gave Gabe a look of raw love, and slipped out of the room.

Three days later, on Sunday afternoon, Gabe's weekend half day off, Collin roared into Guthrie on his motorcycle again and pulled up in front of the diner. The noise of the motorcycle engine brought Gabe to the window of his room and then downstairs to the wooden walk in front of the diner.

Collin didn't have to say anything. He just sat there, on his motorcycle, staring at Gabe. Gabe saddled up behind him on the motorcycle and the two of them rode out to parkland north of town where there were a few small groves of trees running by a riverbed with a trickle of water in it. Gabe had brought a cold six-pack of beer from the diner. After they'd each finished off their third, Collin coaxed Gabe, naked, onto his back, with his legs spread and raised, and Collin, also naked, after sweet-talking Gabe and languidly working Gabe's body with his hands as he would a lover he was coaxing into gentle sex, lowered himself between Gabe's legs. He enclosed Gabe in an entrapping embrace, entered him deep, and, once inside him, set up a vigorous pistoning of his passage. He fucked the shit out of him as Gabe writhed under him, crying out for mercy but receiving none, and, quickly, becoming so taken with the dominating sex not to want mercy.

The next Thursday night, after the diner had closed, Gabe stole silently down to the front door of the diner and let Collin in. Collin had left the motorcycle at the western end of the town so that it didn't alert Sam and his wife, whose apartment was on the first floor at the back, off the kitchen, that he was there. They pulled the mattress off the bed and laid it on the floor so as not to alert Carol, in the next room, with the grinding of the bed against the wall. Collin put Gabe on his belly, coaxed the young man to raise up on his knees a bit to present his pelvis at a good angle, mounted him, and fucked him for nearly an hour. They rested for a half hour, drinking beer Gabe had brought up from the cooler in the diner, and Collin fucked him again for nearly an hour, once in the missionary position and then with Collin on his back and Gabe riding the cock at all four points of the compass. Three hours later, Collin was slipping back out of the front door of the diner. It still was pitch dark outside.

Thus far, Collin was still sampling. He'd paid for practically nothing. Not the beer and not for Gabe's time. He had covered the cost of the gas for the motorcycle, though.

* * * *

Gabe had told Collin it wasn't a good idea, but Collin said he couldn't wait and he wanted to do it in bed, and Gabe hadn't ever been able to tell Collin he couldn't do whatever he wanted to do. Collin was the perpetual dominant and Gabe the total submissive. Gabe had told Collin they'd have to be very quiet as Carol's light was still shining under her door. Collin was sure Carol wouldn't report them to Sam anyway, and so they fucked on the bed.

They'd both had more than one beer too many, and their judgment was impaired. They shushed each other and giggled as they both stripped, not noticing that just the sound of their boots hitting the floorboards reverberated through the building. Once stripped, they almost immediately went into a sixty-nine position, with Collin stretched out along Gabe's body on top of him. Collin's fingers went to Gabe's ass as they sucked each other off and whispered and giggled to each other. It wasn't long until Gabe was on his back, legs spread and bent, arms over his head gripping the brass rungs of the headboard, and his pelvis raised. Collin was kneeling between Gabe's legs, his knees pushed up under Gabe's buttocks. He was hovering over Gabe and looking intensely down into Gabe's eyes. His fists were balled up and pressed into the hollow of Gabe's shoulders on either side of his chest, and Collin was stroking Gabe's channel in long, deep thrusts. The top curve of the headboard was doing a rat-a-tat-tat against the bedroom wall. Carol's bed in the adjacent room was backed to the same wall.

Maybe if either of them was the least bit sober, they would have realized that it wasn't just the shared wall with Carol's room that was being banged, but that it was a noise that could be heard in the middle of the night throughout the structure.

Whether or not it was Carol reporting Gabe had a man in his room, Sam was at the door, using his key to open it when Collin was too far along in fucking Gabe to stop pumping. Sam stood there and watched them finish. He calmly told Collin what the price would be for a go at Gabe. He was still calm when Collin said there had been no agreement to pay and that he'd had Gabe several times before, hadn't paid for it then, and wouldn't pay for it now.

There was some hard eyeballing between the two as Collin pulled his clothes on, but Sam kept his cool and stood aside as Collin walked past him through the door. Sam didn't let him get past, though, without saying, "I don't want to see you around here again—not unless you bring the twenty dollars for this fuck and for every previous fuck and another twenty in advance for the next fuck—and that includes coming to eat at the diner. Let's say $100 will clear the bill. I don't want to see you in there until you've squared the bill."

"I wasn't planning on coming back anyway," Collin growled as he passed by. "I got as much as I want here already."

Gabe felt stung. He forgot all about where he was—that he was naked, in his room, having been discovered doing one of the things that Sam had told him Sam wouldn't tolerate.

"This is being docked from whatever else you make around here," Sam said in a menacing voice. "Two-hundred dollars—twice the price as punishment."

"More than twice as much" Gabe remembered then murmuring absently, "because five dollars of each twenty should be going to me."

He only dredged this up later as what he thought he'd said—without thinking, certainly, as he was quite aware that Sam was wound up tight and barely controlling himself—because at that moment, Sam strode across the floor, raised Gabe, naked, up out of his bed by a one-handed grip on his throat, and proceeded to beat the shit out of him.

Gabe offered little resistance. After the first blow was landed, he was in no condition to fight back. Only the arrival of Sam's wife and Carol and the mention of the danger of killing Gabe got Sam thinking straight.

* * * *

"Ah, here you are, back with us."

Gabe slit his eyes open, batted them to become accustomed to the bright light and then looked into the face of the rancher, Frank Doyle. The face was showing concern. Gabe's own face was swollen and sore, as were his ribs. He had been numbed with something, so the pain was a dull somethingorother in the background, but it was giving notice that as soon as the drugs wore off a bit more, Gabe would be moaning in general body pain.

"Where . . . what?" Gabe murmured through swollen lips, the sound not his voice—something hoarse and thick.

"You're in the doctor's clinic. I brought you over here from the diner. Don't worry, Sam Waller doesn't know you're here. I was in the diner when his wife told me you had been beaten and would I take you out of the building before something worse happened. Sam's over at the sheriff's, giving his story. He says some guy on a motorcycle stole into your room and beat you up last night. But it was Sam, wasn't it?"

"Not the guy who rides the motorcycle," Gabe said, with a groan. "But I won't say—"

"Do you want to go back to the diner—to your room there—to rest? Or do you want to get out of town and away from Sam? If you want to go, you can come back to Sunshine with me. The doctor says he'll give you some painkillers you can take with you that will help until you can take the pain on your own?"

"Back to Sunshine?"

"My ranch. If you don't want to be at the diner when Sam gets back from the sheriff's, you can come out to my ranch until you decide where you want to go, what you want to do. I won't lay a hand on you there . . . if you don't want me too. You won't be in shape to do much of anything for a while anyway. Mrs. Waller has packed up your duffel and I have it here. If there's something else you want that was left at the diner, I could—"

"There's nothing else there I want," Gabe answered. Through swollen eyes, as he lay on the floor after Sam had beaten him, he'd watched Sam find his small stash of cash and pocket it—it didn't come close to the $200 that would satisfy Sam. There was nothing left at the diner to hold Gabe there. He was back to square one again. He looked at Frank, whose stare of concern, longing, and hopefulness would have made Gabe laugh if it wouldn't pain him too much to work his facial muscles. Thinking back on the sex they'd had, he knew that it had been more than just paid sex for Frank. It had been very nice for him too, but Gabe couldn't risk falling into that trap. But, for someplace away from Sam—and even Collin—until he recovered and could get on the road to Lubbock? OK, why the hell not? "I wouldn't mind a bit of sunshine right now," was all he said, before he sank under the influence of the drugs again.

To see Frank's face light up as Gabe was starting to drift off made Gabe embarrassed that he hadn't been more attentive to the man before now—and that he had no intention of giving Frank what he really wanted. Yes, he'd let Frank fuck him when he had recovered, but Frank obviously wanted more. Gabe couldn't afford to want more with Frank. Still, he couldn't not say what he said.

"And, Frank," he said. "If you want to fuck me—whenever you want to fuck me—there'd be no charge."

"It's OK, this isn't the time—" Frank started to say.

"Because I like it from you as much as you do."

Frank smiled at that and patted Gabe on the shoulder. "I'm glad you do—and that you told me."

"If, when we get to your place—to Sunshine—I'm sure we could manage to . . . I'm not hurt where it matters for that."

When they got to Sunshine, they did manage to and, after he'd come after rocking gently with and inside Gabe, Frank left Gabe's bedside with tears in his eyes.

* * * *

Gabe rolled over onto his back from his right side, where just a few minutes before he'd been held close in the embrace of Frank at three points. Frank's knees had been pressed into the fold behind Gabe's knees; Frank's left arm had been slung over Gabe's chest, his hand palming Gabe's right pec; and Frank's cock was buried in Gabe's channel. He had gone flaccid again, but even when soft, he filled Gabe.

The young man had barely recovered before he'd moved to Frank's bed and Frank was covering him nearly every night. It had been Gabe, not Frank, who had pushed this. Gabe knew that Frank was pining for it and he felt the obligation to give Frank what he was too polite to demand for giving him shelter and care. Besides, having been a whore in the diner, Gabe realized that he wanted it regularly. Two of Frank's cowboys, Russell and Lewis, were fucking him too, but that was occasionally, in the barn, and it served to dispel any tension that the rancher was getting in the ranch house what his cowboys couldn't get in the bunkhouse. Gabe didn't throw it into Frank's face that Gabe was giving it to more than him.

They had slept in this position, but before and after that they had fucked. Frank was virile and vigorous for a man in his mid thirties. He was hard as a rock in both muscles and cock. He also was the attentive lover that Gabe had never had before—what Collin had promised to be during initial seduction and then had dropped when he was in the saddle. The more comfortable the two became with the relationship, the more forceful, dominating, inventive, and demanding Frank got with the cocking, although he never was cruel. Gabe tried not to move a muscle, not wanting to do anything that would cause Frank to withdraw from him and rise to the responsibilities of the new day.

Frank was normally an early riser. He had to be to manage this cattle ranch of his north of Guthrie—even though it was a small ranch on the scale of ranches here in northern Texas and even though he had four men to help him. It was past time for him to be up and at it now—and for Gabe to be so, as well, but Gabe didn't want him to go. He wanted to feel the man's wet lips in the hollow of his throat, his fingers start again to pinch and roll Gabe's nipple or descend to his cock, to experience once more the cock coming to life inside him, engorging and filling him to the limit and beginning to move inside him, coaxing him to move with it, for the two of them to become one—for Frank to hold him close, a prisoner, for those times when he was more forceful and demanding, times when Gabe loved losing himself in the heat of Frank's need.

42

As he held his breath, wanting more, even though it was too late in the day to justify the want, especially considering how many times Frank had come and made him come as well in the night, he looked out of the window beside the bed, up into the big blue sky. The sky here, on the Texas plain, was much different from the sky in Louisiana. It was bigger, broader. It even was bluer. In Louisiana it extended in all directions from treetop or from one building to the next. Here in Texas, it extended from horizon to horizon. Here you could actually see that the earth curved.

He sighed as Frank pulled away from him and rolled up, first, into a sitting position on the bed, where Gabe pulled himself up, as well with a groan, and plastered himself to Frank's back, his thighs encompassing Frank's hips, his arms reaching around to palm Frank's pecs and play in the dark body hair swirling there, and his face buried in Frank's throat.

Frank laughed, unwound Gabe's arms, and stood up from the bed. He turned back toward Gabe, and Gabe gasped as he always did when he saw how heavy the rancher was hung. Who would have known that a shy, always modestly dressed, mid-thirties rancher was hung like a bull? Gabe moved to take Frank's cock in his mouth, but, with another low laugh, Frank pulled away from him.

"Later. We both have work to do today," he said. His voice was infused with joy, though, at the relationship that the two men had achieved. It wasn't a partner one—not yet at least. Frank knew that two of his hired hands, Russell and Lew, had fucked Gabe too since he'd come to the ranch. But that was happening less and less and he felt that he and Gabe were coming closer together. It was only a matter of time, he hoped, before they could become what he wanted—partners, Frank dominant, of course, and Gabe submissive. He had hopes that Gabe would be with him only, but he understood what Gabe had come from, recognized that Gabe was highly sexed, and had the patience to wait for a deeper relationship to develop.

"I want you to go to the south quarter with Russell today and count how many head we have down there— keeping a separate count of ones ready to go to market. It's nearly time to make up another shipment for the Omaha stock yards," Frank said. The Union Stockyards, here in the mid fifties, had become the premier destination for cattle across the West. "I have to pick up a shipment of the feed supplement in Lubbock I've ordered for some of the ranches around here and deliver it."

He had been padding around the bedroom, naked, and gathering the clothes together for the day. It had only been recently that he had overcome his modesty and walked around naked in front of Gabe. He was doing so at Gabe's request. Gabe had told him how beautiful his body was. Frank apparently hadn't been aware of that before. He didn't know that he was hung like a bull until Gabe told him—or that young men would lay down for a man with a big cock. He hadn't made the effort to compare himself to other men. But knowing that Gabe became aroused at seeing him swing free encouraged him to be nude in the house more.

It also encouraged him to play with himself. Before he had masturbated in private, in the dark, and only by necessity of relieving tension, embarrassed that he was compelled to do it. Gabe said he enjoyed watching Frank masturbate, so he was doing it in front of Gabe more. He had also learned not to feel guilty or embarrassed when Gabe sucked it—or when he sucked Gabe's cock. He was learning to revel in sex.

He noticed that Gabe's eyes were downcast.

"Is something wrong, Gabe?" he asked. "Did you want to go with me to Lubbock today? Did you want to try again to find your friend?"

"No, no, everything's fine," Gabe said, looking up and producing, with a bit of effort, a smile. "Checking out the south quarter is just fine." He didn't want to reveal that it was going out on the range with Russell was what wasn't all that fine. Having become satisfied with and feeling safe with Frank in bed, Gabe had started denying other guys—he didn't need the extra money now, either, as he'd given up on the Lubbock idea—but Russell hadn't been as cooperative with that as Lew had been.

Life thus far at Sunshine Ranch had been complicated for Gabe, but it was all starting to settle down. Although the ranch had a bunkhouse for the hired hands, Gabe had been put in a bedroom in the main house when Frank had brought him from Guthrie—and he remained in the main house even after recovering and starting to work for Frank.

Frank had cared for him for two weeks until he could comfortably walk again and then had offered him a temporary job.

"I know you told me you were just passing through on your way to Lubbock," he'd said, "but one of my men, Art, has had to go off because his mother is having a rough time dying and I don't know when he'll be back. It takes five men to run this place. If you can stay on for a while, you could fill in for Art until he gets back. And maybe you could use the money I'd pay you. We'd see what was what then. I don't really want you to leave—unless that's what you want."

Gabe had been waiting for Frank to say what other way than sex Gabe could earn money from him. He knew Frank wanted to fuck him—once or twice a day if he didn't restrain himself. And he'd tentatively brought this up.

"Sure, I can fill in for your guy, but is that really how you want me to earn my keep here? You've been great to me. I want you to have what you want. You want me to remain here in the house, or, if I'm going to work the ranch, do you want me to move over to the bunkhouse?"

"I want you to stay in the house," Frank answered in a hoarse voice. He didn't follow that up, though, and he didn't look at Gabe directly.

Gabe had had to take matters into his own hands. That night, he came, naked, into Frank's bedroom. He pulled the sheet off of Frank to find that the man too was naked—and Gabe gasped at seeing how hard bodied he was and hung. Frank had been furtive with him the few times they'd fucked before, not letting Gabe see what Frank was putting in his ass. Once they had started into it, Gabe taking Frank's cock in his mouth and running his hands over Frank's body and, when Frank was hard and groaning, positioning his channel over Frank's cock, sinking on it, and riding it to a mutual ejaculation, Frank showed, for the rest of the night, that he was ready, willing, and very, very able.

After that, there increasingly was less and less awkwardness between the two and no possessiveness either. When Art came back after Gabe had been there for six weeks and, over three weeks, had worked his way into full-time duties on the ranch, nothing was said of Gabe not having a job. Frank said nothing, either, about Gabe going with both Russell and Lew for money or, more often, establishment of good will on occasion, although he surely knew this was happening. After Gabe had been there for two months, Frank brought Lubbock up.

"You have said you have someone to go to in Lubbock," he said. "You probably have saved up enough money to get there now, but if you want to go, I'll drive you there." This obviously meant that Frank knew Gabe was making money on the side and also knew the most likely way Gabe was making the money. Although he paid Gabe for his work on the ranch, it wasn't much, as room and board were included.

Gabe was taken aback that Frank would be so willing for him to move on, but he hid as best he could that this hurt him a bit. Indeed, he didn't realize that he would be hurt that Frank was willing for him to leave until Frank mentioned it. It wasn't until now that Gabe realized that he was growing as close to Frank as he was.

"You'd drive me there?" he said, trying not to look disappointed. "Yes, that's what I'd like then." If Frank didn't think they were becoming close—that Gabe was just a nice, convenient lay—then maybe it was best Gabe moved on, he thought. He realized he'd been dropping hints of Russell and Lew fucking him to see if it would get a rise out of Frank. But it didn't. Frank wasn't the least bit possessive of Gabe. He didn't criticize his lifestyle or his promiscuity or hem him in in any way.

There was no way for Gabe to know that this only was because Frank was afraid of losing him.

The road trip to Lubbock had been a disaster for Gabe, though. Frank drove him into the center of the city and stopped at a telephone booth.

"Maybe you want to call him before we go there," Frank said. In his mind, from what Gabe had said about this Adrian friend of his, the guy sounded like a real player. Frank didn't think he would have waited for Gabe to show up on his doorstep even though he'd invited Gabe to join him.

And Frank turned out to be right. The telephone call got someone speaking Spanish and not producing anyone else when Gabe provided the name of Adrian.

"OK, we tried advance notice. I'll drive you on over there. Now that we're here, I know you won't want to leave without being sure."

"Over there," turned out to be a three-story adobe apartment house in a seedy part of town. And those at the apartment address Adrian had given were still solely Spanish speakers. The super, though, answering the door of the apartment marked as the office, was quite happy to see them and focused his attention on Gabe.

"Lover boy Adrian? He got in with some guys making TV commercials and other kinds of movies. They liked what he'd do and took him off to tinsel town. He's in L.A., I think. You look like the film guys would like you too. Maybe you could follow him out there. You want, I'll put you in contact with them. You could stay with me until you're set up if you'd like. I'd like. Adrian and I got along real well. Real well, if you know what I mean."

Both Gabe and Frank knew what the guy meant. He was a little greasy but he wasn't a slob. Gabe knew what was behind the leer he was giving him. He hesitated. He didn't see much in the way of options.

"You could come home with me—back to Sunshine," Frank said.

Was that a tone of hopefulness or "put-upon" resignation in Frank's voice, Gabe wondered.

"I don't know. I can't live off your generosity forever he said."

"It's not generosity, Gabe. It's deeper than that. I'd like you to come home with me."

Gabe looked up at the sky. Even here in Lubbock, everything looked flat. Everything was covered by a big, deep-blue sky. "I guess we could give it a try," he said, "if I wouldn't be too much of an imposition for you."

When they got back to the Sunshine Ranch, Frank showed Gabe how much of an imposition it wouldn't be. They stayed in Frank's bed for a day and a half, while Frank showed Gabe that lovemaking went way beyond mere fucking.

* * * *

"You know it won't take all day to do the cattle count on the south quarter," Russell said as he and Gabe rode out from the ranch compound on horses. Gabe was surprised they hadn't taken the Jeep, but Russell had said the south quarter actually had some hills and gullies where water ran into a shallow river during the wet season, making Jeep travel problematic. There were some places on the ranch that could only be reached by horseback. Gabe hadn't been to that quarter of Sunshine and hadn't really seen much in the way of hills and gullies in Texas yet, and he hadn't experienced a rainy season here.

"In the rainy season, we could get some real gushers where we're going," Russell said. "No place for a vehicle then. Caught by a gusher, we could be out there cut off from the rest of the world for days, just the two of us. How would you like that, Gabe—all alone out there for me a couple of days? We'd have time for me to do you royally. How would you like that?"

"Yeah, that would be something, Russ."

"You're pretty much with Frank now, right?"

"Right, Russ."

"But we really had it on, didn't we? I can't think of Frank giving you what I gave you."

Gabe wondered what Russell would do or say if Gabe told him that Frank had two more inches to give him than Russell did. And, like a lot of submissives, inches counted with Gabe. Russell had a short fuse. A little bit of crazy, Russell was.

"We really got it on, didn't we?" the cowboy continued. "You'd like some more of that, I'll bet. There are some cottonwoods by the river where we're going. Some shade. I brought some beer. The ice packs should

49

hold till we get to the river. We can do the count later. And, yeah, I brought money. I know you do it for the money."

There wasn't much more to say. Russell was a big bruiser. He outweighed Gabe by a good sixty pounds— sixty pounds of muscle. And Russell had gotten it from Gabe before. It's not like Gabe didn't do it for money and hadn't done it with Russell before for money. It was clear that Russell was going to do him, money or no money.

And Russell was right about doing guys like Frank never had or would. Russell had a mean streak in him and that's how he did it.

Russell fucked Gabe in the shade of a grove of cottonwood trees on the bank of a shallow river running through a gully that indicated that, when the rains came, it would hardly contain a raging torrent.

Russell fucked Gabe hard and vigorously and bound and then he slapped him around and whipped him. He just tended to beat the young man enough to help make Russell hard. He knew better than to main the boss's poke. Once started, it was hard to maintain control, though.

Gabe had gotten a taste of the cowboy's cruelty before but nothing like this. Being out in the raw, arid wilderness like this brought a heightened sense of power and wild-man entitlement to the big, leather-skinned brute. On top of this, he had leave to play out his resentment that Gabe got to sleep in the main house, under the rancher, even though he was a rent-boy and that he'd been avoiding Russell. Well, Russell's money was as good as Frank's, his cocking was a damn sight more interesting, Russell believed, and he was as much a man as Gabe could take.

He put Gabe, naked, belly over a saddle resting on the ground, tied off the young man's wrists, his arms over his head, with a leather strap wrapped around the base of a young cottonwood tree, and he had Gabe's legs spread and staked out. He mounted Gabe's ass from above and behind and rode him hard.

"You love it, don't you?"

"Yes, yes, I love it," Gabe cried out—and embarrassingly, he did.

He didn't love it so much when Russell laid into him with a hand whip, striking him on the back, buttocks, and thighs. But Russell didn't put his full force behind his strikes, and the welts he'd left Gabe with would have done nothing more than sting for a while if then, after Russell mounted and fucked him again, they hadn't had to ride the section and do the cattle count they'd been sent out there to do.

"You're walking gingerly," Frank said when they returned and Gabe climbed the stairs of the ranch house. "Saddle sores? I would have thought you'd be used to the saddle by now."

"Yeah, saddle sores," Gabe mumbled as he passed Frank and went into the ranch house. He wasn't about to tell him all that had happened out there in the south quarter. He had to fit in in this outfit. Russell was the senior cowboy here. And Russell had paid him well for what Russell got. Gabe would just have to suck it up—and try to avoid being alone with Russell in the future. "I just haven't done as much riding before as I had to do today," he said as he disappeared into the ranch house. Or been ridden as hard, he added in his mind.

Frank sensed something was wrong, though, and followed Gabe into the house. As Gabe was going to the shower, Frank came into the bathroom and saw the welts on the young man's back, buttocks, and thighs.

"You didn't get that from riding a horse," he said. "Russell did that to you, didn't he?"

Gabe turned and gave Frank a scared look. "I don't want to cause trouble at the ranch, Frank. I want to fit in. I'll figure this out."

"I want you to fit in too," Frank said. He turned and walked back to the living room and to the gun safe, which he opened. Gabe came in as he was taking a rifle out of the case.

"No, Frank. You don't want to do this. I'm a whore. Russell didn't take anything away from me that I haven't given other men. He paid for it."

"You gave him a price for letting him whip you?"

"Not exactly."

"Other men have flogged you?" Frank asked.

"Not yet . . . not other than Russell. You saw how Sam beat me, though."

"Sam didn't do it to have sex with you, to get hard and to jack off from breaking you. He just couldn't control his anger at something you did that he told you not to do."

"Just don't do anything on my account," Gabe said. He didn't want to say that he'd enjoyed most of what Russell had done with him. "He paid for it, Frank. I took the money. I'm trying to cut down on anyone other than you. But if you want, I'll leave. You need Russell here more than you need me."

"You don't know, do you?" Frank said, his voice shaking. "You still don't know where you fit in at this ranch. Don't worry, I won't shoot him. I just want to motivate him."

Within the hour, Russell was packed up and gone.

When Frank came back into the house, he made Gabe, who had showered by now, lay on his belly on the bed and he dressed his welts with salve.

"You just can't seem to understand it," he murmured, "but there's no one in this world I need here more than you." He had wanted to say this to Gabe for weeks, but he knew Gabe was a free spirit—that he'd have agreed to go with Russell today showed that he still wasn't tamed. And Frank didn't know as he ever wanted Gabe to be tamed. He hadn't had the courage to tell Gabe before how fully he was invested in the young man. And it didn't mean much in telling him now. Gabe had drifted off to sleep.

He didn't use the "love" word. But Gabe wasn't dumb. He didn't need the word to be spoken now. He just wasn't ready to say the word himself.

~

Chapter Four: Make You a Movie Star

Looking back on it, Frank Doyle could have kicked himself for asking Gabe if he'd like to go along on the delivery of sacks of feed supplements to the Brighton Ranch. He'd had no idea that they were filming a movie there and he had no idea who was involved in the movie or that the ranch's manager, Sterling Fisher, had been one of Gabe's clients at the Lone Star Diner in Guthrie.

They were at one of the barns, within sight of the huge, rambling, weather-beaten wood Victorian main house that stood out on the flat arid land like some sort of alien spaceship plunked down in a desert. They were unloading feed bags from the back of Frank's pickup truck and wondering what all of the activity and unusual equipment surrounding the house, with its incongruous patch of grass lawn out front, was about when Frank went stiff. Gabe turned to see what Frank was looking at, taking a few seconds to understand why Frank looked so shocked and concerned.

There was a fancy convertible sitting in front of the ranch house—not really a ranch house; more a displaced Victorian mansion. It was a 1954 Ford Sunliner convertible, two tone yellow and white. Perched on the top of the driver's seat was a young sunny blonde woman in a frilly yellow dress with white trimmings. And standing on the ground beside her, with an arm around her waist and all trimmed out in black leather faux cowboy apparel was . . .

Collin Chisholm, Gabe's motorcycle lover from the Lone Star Diner. Three photographers were circling them, taking still shots.

"Isn't that—?" Frank started to ask.

"Yes. I wonder what's going on?" Gabe said.

Further speculation was short circuited when a small, emaciated woman with owl eyes and owl eyeglasses dominating her face, showed up, holding a clipboard, and said, "All of the extras are gathering over there near the horse corral."

"We're not extra, Ma'am," Frank said, with a smile, tipping his cowboy hat at the woman. "But can you tell us what's going on over at the house?"

"Filming a movie. *Big Sky Country*," she said, a cigarette wagging at the corner of her mouth. "An A movie. Epic. A Texas family goes from dirt ranching to millionaires in two generations and very nearly to pot after that. Those are publicity shots. Most of the 'before' part has already been filmed. The oil wells go in next week. We're about to go on hiatus from the house remodeling."

"And those people—the girl in the convertible and the cowpoke?" Frank followed up.

"Pamela Barker. Surprised you don't recognize her. This year's ingénue bombshell. The daughter of the family. The young man is Collin Chisholm, up and coming heartthrob. On the porch, talking to who I don't know is Jay Jones, box office cash register and heartthrob of two decades ago. Jones is playing the family patriarch. Susan Tyler, leading lady, just flies in for her scenes and then flies back to California. The production had to lease a plane just for her. You sure you two aren't here to play extras? You're both perfect for it."

"The other man on the porch is Sterling Fisher," Frank said. "He lives in that house. But, no, Ma'am, I'm just here to deliver feed. Maybe Gabe here, though . . ."

55

He turned and looked at Gabe and his heart flipped up into his throat. The suggestion was the very last thing he should have said, he immediately recognized. Gabe had the star-struck look in his eyes and his gaze was fixed on Collin Chisholm, who had now seen them and was walking toward them, his eyes on Gabe.

"What's entailed in being an extra in this movie?" Gabe asked.

Gabe was so taken with exchanging looks with Collin that he didn't notice that the men on the porch—the ranch manager and major stockholder, Sterling Fisher, and the handsome, mature leading actor, Jay Jones, were now also looking at him. Fisher was talking, and Jones was smiling.

* * * *

"No, it's fine if you stay here until they don't need you any more for filming," Frank said, his voice sounding enthusiastic but the look he was giving Gabriel didn't match that. Gabriel, who had gotten the name upgrade when the casting woman decided that's what she'd write on her clipboard because it sounded better as a movie name, was starry eyed and looking at the activity going on around him, his gaze constantly going back to Collin Chisholm, rather than to Frank.

"There's probably room in the bunkhouse," the casting woman said, her cigarette wagging at the corner of her mouth, although she sounded a bit dubious. "Never can tell when we need the extras to form up, so it would be best if you were here when you were needed."

"He can bunk in my trailer," Collin Chisholm chimed in, with a smile. This made Frank's brow knit a little deeper, but the casting woman seemed to be cheered by the offer, completely indifferent to the dynamics that were playing out.

"See costuming over there in that barn," she said, turning to the newly minted Gabriel, the housing issue being solved as far as she was concerned. "They'll have the last word on what you wear in the scenes where you're background, but I wouldn't be surprised if they decide you are perfect just the way you are."

"Yeah, I think he's perfect just the way he is," Collin said, giving Gabriel the eye.

Turning toward the truck, Frank said, "I'll bring your stuff back when I deliver the next load of feed later this afternoon." It wasn't clear whether either Gabriel or Collin heard him, though, as Collin had a hand on Gabriel's forearm and was already moving out to show him to the actor's trailer.

As the male heartthrob second lead in the motion picture, Collin rated one of the bigger trailers. There were three compartments—the central compartment included the living area off to one side and a kitchenette and L-shaped bench, with a dining table, off to the other side. A short hallway, with a closet on one side, and a small bathroom, with shower on the other, led from the kitchen/dining space to a bedroom at the back of the trailer that was dominated by a double bed. Up front, off the living area, a small compartment accommodated two bunk beds and a built-in armoire.

Gabriel was shown the bunk beds after Collin had bent him over the dining table and fucked him doggie style, but later Gabriel was fucked on Collin's double bed at the other end of the trailer, with the new movie extra on his back, grasping the rungs of the headboard over his head, legs spread and bent and pelvis thrusting up to receive Collin's downward thrusts of his cock. Collin hovered over Gabriel's body, his fists buried in the mattress on either side of the young man's shoulders, and pumped and pumped and pumped.

Gabriel allowed as how the accommodations and hospitality attention would be just fine with him.

* * * *

As it turned out, extras, including Gabe, weren't going to be needed for much longer. Filming of the early-years phase of the movie was coming to a close. Before they could move to the "years later" phase, the house needed to be completely redone and the husks of oil well pumpjacks had to be dotted over the nearby landscape. The scenes already in the can had been filmed piecemeal, with an eye to the ongoing project needs of the actors, and all but one of Collin's scenes were finished already. Collin was actually in the "years later" portion of the film but he had another movie to go to and the magic of film editing would change his backgrounds. After this, there would just be this or that short take filmed of the early phase. Gabriel had learned this as soon as Collin took him to his trailer. Collin was already stripping off his shirt as they entered.

"Get comfortable, which means strip down, while I get a couple of beers," he said. "Then I want you to suck me off and I'll do you."

"Just like that?" Gabriel asked—with a smile, though, because he had no objection to Collin fucking him. He'd missed Collin. "No showing me where I'm to bunk or anything?"

"You bunk through that door there, and you can put your clothes there now, if you want, but for the short time I'm here, you'll probably be under me on my bed, which is that direction. Here's your beer. You aren't naked yet. Get a move on, lad. Time is short."

"Time is short?"

"Yeah. My last scene films this afternoon. Another day or two and I'm back in Hollywood. Just have to make arrangements on the shipping of my Harley."

"The movie is folding up?"

"My part of it is, but there will be time for you to be filmed. Some of the background stuff is still to be shot. What we don't have much time to do is fuck, and I've been thinking of you. On your knees. Give me good head."

Gabriel dutifully went on his knees between Collin's spread thighs as the actor sprawled on the built-in sofa. Gabriel gave him head while Collin swigged his beer and told Gabriel what he liked from the suck and what he liked more. When Collin was good and stiff, he just bent Gabriel over the table between the kitchenette and the bench, worked his cock inside Gabriel's ass, grasped the young man's hips with his hands, and started pumping him. This obviously was fine with Gabriel, who went completely docile as Collin spiked him and extended his arms straight out from his sides in a cruciform position and grasped the edge of the table top to hold himself steady under the rhythm of the fuck.

A couple of hours later they were out next to the corral, where the breakup scene of the second part of the movie was filmed between Collin's character and that of the young blonde character being played by Pamela Baker. At the beginning of the scene the two characters were in an embrace, leaning on the fender of the Baker character's yellow convertible and watching a horse being exercised in the corral. Gabriel was the cowpoke exercising the horse, and he was grateful that he'd been cowpoking on the Sunshine Ranch long enough to learn how to exercise a horse like this.

The scene drifted into a heated conversation between the two leaning against the convertible, as Gabriel continued calmly exercising the horse in the ring. The argument got so heated that the Collin character jumped into the convertible and roared off. In the movie, down the road, he would wrap himself around a pole and disappear from the movie two-thirds of the way to the film's end. Back at the corral, the brazen little blonde, pretending that it was good riddance for the Collin character, would come to the railing of the corral and give the cowpoke exercising the horse a come-hither look. It would already have been established that the young woman was a vixen who opened her legs to any man she fancied. The scene would end with Gabriel's character meeting her gaze and walking toward her. This was 1955, so there wouldn't be more to the scene than that, but the audience would understand that the two went off and fucked.

It was a short, straightforward scene, but they did so many takes of it that Gabriel wasn't all that enthused about working in movies when the director was finally satisfied that they had what they could use. Pamela Barker, though, was impressed enough to give him the come-hither looks off camera that she'd given him on camera. He was polite but there was no way he was going to give her a toss in the hay when Collin was fucking him as well as he was.

Collin drove the yellow convertible back for the last time and switched over to his motorcycle, saying that he had to ride it in to Lubbock to turn over to the shipping company and would see Gabriel after dinner—that they'd both been invited up to the big house for a party that evening.

"I'll go back to the trailer for a shower and a nap, then," Gabriel said. "I think that horse kicked up half of Texas on me while we were going through all of those takes."

"I guess I can take the Harley back a little later then," Collin said, with a smile and a wink. "A shower sounds good to me too."

Unless she was really a dumb blonde, Pamela Barker got the lay of the land with Gabriel as she watched the two men strut off toward Collin's trailer, with Collin pulled in close to Gabriel and guiding the young man with a hand on the small of his back.

The shower in the trailer was small, but the two men managed in there together just fine, Gabriel's back against the wall under the shower head, his arms flung around Collin's neck and his legs hooked on Collin's hips, as the actor moved Gabriel's body up and down on the wall with the thrusts of his cock.

* * * *

Gabriel stood on the front porch for quite some time waiting for Collin to show up to take him into the main house at the Brighton Ranch. It had been Collin who had told him there was to be a party here and that they were invited. But Collin hadn't shown up yet and no one else had passed Gabriel to go into the house for the party. Maybe he'd gotten the message wrong, he thought. It had been OK as he stood at the porch railing and watched the sun go down, but now he was just standing there—in the dark. He was skittish about coming to the house, because Sterling Fisher lived here and he'd been one of Gabriel's regular clients upstairs at the Lone Star Diner in Guthrie. And Fisher had been a rough and vigorous fucker. Most important, he knew that Gabriel was a rent-boy.

He was about to give up on Collin and go back to the trailer, thinking that Collin must have had some problem about the shipping company in Lubbock taking his motorcycle, when the front door opened and Sterling Fisher, a tall and big man, loomed inside the doorframe, highlighted by the light spilling out from the large foyer back by a massive staircase.

"How long you been out here . . . Gabe, isn't it?" Fisher asked a gruff voice. He was wearing a silk bathrobe—just that—and had a can of Bud beer in his hand. "Where's Collin?"

Looking past Fisher, it looked like everything in the downstairs of the house was dark. The man was in his robe. Obviously Gabriel had gotten the timing of the party wrong.

"Sorry, Mr. Fisher, I think I got it wrong. You look like you are about to go to bed. I thought there was a party here tonight. Collin said he'd meet me here, but he's not here."

"Well, we can go on without Collin," Fisher said. "You got the party right. Come on in. Here." He extended the beer can toward Gabriel and Gabriel took it. "There's more where that came from. Come on in." He stood aside so that Gabriel could slip past him and into the house. But still Gabriel hesitated.

"You look like you're about to go to bed."

"We'll get around to the bed. But I'm so keyed up I'll fuck you on the floor first—on a bearskin rug in front of the fireplace, just like in the movies." And then when Gabriel gave him a blank stare, Fisher laughed and said, "You mean Collin didn't tell you that you were the entertainment for this intimate party? I know men fuck you. I've fucked you myself and am in the mood to do it again. Get your tail in here, strip off those clothes, and let's get to it. I know the price you go for. You'll get paid." He opened the sash to his robe, which parted to show that he was in massive erection.

Gabriel got fucked doggie style on a bearskin rug in front of a fire in a massive stone fireplace in the mansion's living room—just as promised. Fisher was as hung and rough and vigorous and long lasting as he had been on

Gabe's squeaking bed on the second floor of the Lone Star Diner in Guthrie.

The young man's tail was high in the air, supported on his knees, his chest was flat on the bearskin rug, his arms were extended over his head, and his cheek were pressed into the fur, his mouth open in a silent scream and his eyes gazing into the burning logs. The older man was long and thick and in superb condition. Gabe knew it would be a long, taxing ride. And he knew that he had no choice but to endure it. This was Fisher's ranch, Fisher's money was on the table in front of the sofa, and they both knew that Gabriel went with men for money.

Fisher was the sort of man who was going to take Gabriel if he wanted to whether or not Gabriel wanted it. It just prevented it being an ordeal if Gabriel went with the flow.

Fisher rode him high, like he was a jockey on a race, standing in a crouch hovering over his back. The similarity to a jockey was pronounced at first as he had a hand whip and laid into Gabriel's back and buttocks as he was building up speed of the thrust. Quickly, though, he'd tossed the whip aside—before he had raised much in the way of welts—and covered Gabriel close from above, his fists clutching Gabriel's wrists, his teeth latching onto the back of Gabriel's neck, and his pelvis thrusting a mile a minute until Gabriel groaned and came. A full two minutes of riding later, Fisher jerked, creamed Gabriel's channel deep, and pulled out of him. He pushed the young man over on his side, back to the fireplace, and sat, wide stanced, cock hanging low, on a footstool beside Gabriel, and took a deep swig from a can of Bud.

"That was as good as I remembered—better because this room is a big step up from the one you have at the Lone Star—and we'll do that again real soon," Fisher said in a low voice, "but that's not what this party is about."

Gabriel just lay there, staring at the man, unkinking his limbs, thinking about whether anyone had been deeper inside him before than this man could reach.

"I need to know if you can be totally discreet if the money is right."

"I never told nobody you came for me at the diner," Gabriel answered.

"It's not about me. It's about someone else who's seen you and wants you—but that it can't be known he likes men. You get taken care of right, can you keep it a secret?"

"Nobody's had a reason to say otherwise," Gabriel answered. "But . . ."

"He's upstairs. He's the one who wanted this party. He'll give you $200 for the night and your silence. You blab and he'll ruin your life and you'll be giving up the opportunity for more good money. Understand?"

"Yes, I guess so."

"You'll accept and keep your yap buttoned about it?"

"Yes," Gabriel said, starting to rise from the rug.

"I didn't say you could get up. I said I'd do you again real soon. Real soon is now. First crawl over here and clean my cock. Then I want you to shower and I'll send you in to him."

Gabriel rose on his knees between Fisher's spread legs and took the cock in his mouth. Then he took the cock in his ass, sitting on it, facing Fisher and arched back, palms reversed on the floor, as Fisher grasped his hips and pulled him on off his cock to their mutual second ejaculation.

* * * *

Jay Jones, the leading man of the movie being filmed, *Big Sky Country*, was an experienced and attentive

64

lover. It was quite clear that he had had many men before. He wasn't fully hard bodied and he was older than he filmed as or even as he looked stretched out on the bed with his cock in his hand. He probably was pushing hard toward fifty, but he looked to be in his early forties, and, though his body was mature, it was toned and had not gone to fat. He was muscular enough to manipulate Gabriel's smaller, lithe body easily and expertly, and he was well tanned, the whiter tone of his bathing suit lines accentuating his Zeus-form musculature. He was uncommonly—almost plastically—handsome, in keeping with being a leading man movie star, with wavy black hair on his head, curling around his pecks, and descending in a thin line into his trimmed pubes—and then curling on his thighs as well.

"Just relax and let me take care of everything," he had said, "we have all night." And when Gabe had given in to that, all had gone smoothly and Gabe's needs had all been taken care of—repeatedly, through the night. This was not a quickie fuck.

Jones's cock wasn't noticeably long, although it filled out nicely when hard and remained hard until it had exhausted Gabriel. He may have been on some sort of enhancement drug to maintain his erection. The shaft was thick, and Jones knew what to do with it to make Gabriel pant and moan and beg for more of it. His balls were plump and full of cum, which he slowly doled out to Gabriel all night on the big bed in a bedroom outfitted like a scarlet-decorated Victorian bordello.

He worked Gabriel's body for three-quarters of an hour before fucking him, fondling the young man to a heavy pant, kissing and tonguing him everywhere, and getting four fingers inside him and working his prostate until with a groan and a cry for mercy Gabriel released his cum and rolled over onto his belly in exhaustion. Then and only then did Jones cover the younger man's body closely from above, grasp Gabriel's wrists with his hands, bury his face in the hollow of the young man's throat, enter him slowly and deeply, and slow-pump him to an ejaculation, to Gabe's gasps and their mutual groans and moans. When Jones came the first time, both men were lying perfectly still except for rise and fall of Jones's hips and the almost imperceptible rise of Gabriel's pelvis to meet the slow thrusts.

Jones took him a second time in a missionary and a third time in a side split, and before the light of dawn began to filter through the cracks in the scarlet velvet draperies on the tall windows, Gabriel coaxed the older man onto his back and slowly rode his cock in a cowboy, ending with Jones pulling him back onto his torso, trapping his arms in a full nelson, weaving his legs through Gabriel's, and fucking up into his ass, ending in yet another prodigious coming by the actor and Gabriel splashing his cum up onto his belly. As far as Gabriel could figure out, the actor remained in erection the entire time.

They went to sleep like that, with Gabe lying on top of Jones's stretched-out body and Jones's at last flaccid cock inside Gabe's channel.

The sun had breached the horizon when they both woke to pounding on the front door downstairs and to the sound of Sterling Fisher going down to answer the door.

When he came upstairs, he tapped on the bedroom door and opened it before either Jones or Gabriel could answer. He of course saw the two men plastered together on top of sheets that were all askelter, but he gave this no reaction. It wasn't anything less than he expected to find.

"There's a reason Collin didn't come to the party last night," he said, his voice flat and ominous. "On the way into Lubbock yesterday, he rammed a telephone pole head on with his motorcycle and killed himself."

Gabriel gave a sob, rolled off Jones's body, and sat on the side of the bed, his body sunk in on itself.

"I guess it's good that his last scene was shot yesterday," Fisher added.

Gabriel sobbed again and hiccupped. Jones hissed a, "That's enough of that, Sterling," to Fisher, who shrugged, withdrew, and closed the door behind him.

Jones rolled over to the side of the bed and came in close behind Gabriel, encasing the young man's thighs between his and embracing Gabriel's torso in his arms. He kissed the shocked young man on the neck and shoulders and rocked him back and forth.

"Go ahead, let it out," he whispered, and Gabriel did so for a few minutes.

When the shudders and sobs subsided a bit, Jones whispered, in his best calming stage voice, "It's terrible that Collin is gone. But he went doing what he wanted—riding with the wind on his motorcycle. He's gone, but you are here and so am I. You are young and supple, at the height of your desirability. You have so much to live for and so much more to enjoy in life. I want you to come to Hollywood with me. We'll take Collin back and put him to rest in Forest Lawn. I will be good to you. I want to be good to you. I want to be good to you now. Grasp life. Let me have you again. Now. It will comfort you to affirm life like this. Move up and come down on me—take me inside you. I will be good to you." He was a consummate actor. He knew just how to pitch his voice in a soothing, encouraging tone.

With a stifled sob, Gabriel rose enough on his feet, planted on the floor, to let Jones put his erect cock, which had engorged while they'd been rocking their bodies against each other, in position. With a sigh Gabriel descended on the cock and then, with Jones embracing him from behind, he turned his head for their faces to meet in a kiss and began to rise and fall on the buried shaft.

Jay Jones cooed in soft tones to the young man and stroked the curves of his body as he fucked him again. Jones was getting what he wanted from the young man, and Gabriel, young, naïve, and awed at coupling with a famous actor, submitted fully to him.

* * * *

The next afternoon, after Collin Chisholm's coffin had been loaded onto the productions Douglas DC-5 aircraft at the Lubbock airport and they'd taken off, Gabriel sat at a window and looked down at the out-of-place Victorian mansion on the Brighton Ranch, as the aircraft circled to head West.

"How long will we be in Hollywood before we come back here?" he turned and asked Jay Jones, who was sitting in the aisle seat on the other side of the plane and looking over a script.

"Oh, we won't be back for months," Jones said. "They have to modernize the house, paint it all up, and add gardens and a pool for the latter years section of the movie. It's what the ranch gets done to let us film there. That will take months."

"Months? We'll be gone for months? Not just a week or so to get Collin buried?"

"No. Months. We have scenes we can shoot at Studio City, and I'm in discussions on a movie down in Mexico I could get started on. If that doesn't pan out, there is plenty of publicity work to do. Don't worry. You'll be with me. I'll take very good care of you."

Gabriel turned back to the window and looked down to see if he could pick out Frank Doyle's Sunshine Ranch. He hadn't had time to tell Frank he was going back

68

to Hollywood with Collin's body to see him buried. He felt someone slip into the aisle seat beside him and turned to see a dark-haired man of thirty-five or so. Not bad looking but a little on the pudgy side. He remembered having seen him at the ranch but didn't know what his job was on the movie.

Jay Jones told him. "This is Sam Lutz, Gabe. He's an assistant producer on the picture. Keeps track of the filming schedules."

Then he told Gabriel why Sam Lutz was smiling at him. "He asked about you. Heard you gave twenty-five-dollar blow jobs. I figured you could use the money. You can do it right there, or if you'd like more privacy, I think the last row in the cabin is free." Then he turned his attention back to reading the script in his lap.

It went beyond a blow job. Eventually, Gabriel's bare legs were raised, spread, and waving out over the top of the row of seats in front of him, with Lutz crouched between them, fucking Gabriel. No one on the plane seemed to notice, or, if they did, to care. It did take much for Gabriel to be clear what function he was to perform in the film production entourage.

~

Chapter Five: Hollywood Ho

Gabriel—even Jay Jones insisted that Gabe call himself Gabriel now—didn't know why Jay insisted that he come to this concert. He wasn't a concert sort of person—or at least wasn't until Jay took on the crusade of refining him. Even then Jay didn't usually want them to be seen at the same concert. Gabriel was the actor's hidden boy toy. He particularly didn't like Latin music. But then, as the studio executive, Julio Martinez, came down the aisle, necessitating that Gabriel stand at his seat to let him pass in the row, and then sat down in the seat beside Gabriel and gave him a knowing little smile, Gabriel reminded himself that he did know why he was here.

"Here" was the Hollywood Bowl amphitheater on a warm and star-encrusted—both in the heavens and in the theater—August 18th, 1955, night. The venue was the third day of the Festival of the Americas, organized by the composer and conductor Leonard Bernstein as musical director. It was Latin night, and the Los Angeles Orchestra was playing Latin music under the baton of Mexican conductor and composer, Carlos Chavez. It had been four months since Gabriel had flown away from Lubbock, Texas, not realizing he was being spirited away permanently by Jay Jones, four months during which he had lived in secret in a cottage at the back of Jones's Beverly Hills estate, coming and going through the rear alley. And it had been four months in which Jay Jones had trained him to serve Jay Jones—both underneath Jay Jones and with other men to the benefit of Jones's career.

Gabriel was in the section that could be called the "better" seats in the amphitheater. That was because of the man who had just entered and sat down beside him—Julio Martinez, the movie studio's connection with Mexico, who handled everything needed in the way of support south of the border. Martinez was in the "better" seating section because he was one of the sponsors of this particular concert. Jay Jones was here tonight, but he made sure he was never seen in public with Gabriel. He was in the "best" seating section, escorting for the evening the stage and movie star, Mary Martin, who had just completed a two-week run in *Skin of Our Teeth* at L.A.'s Blackstone Theater. Gabriel was here, in this seat, because of Martinez. That he was at the concert at all was because Martinez had told Jay Jones about a movie to be filmed in Mexico that Jones wanted to star in, and Martinez had told Jones what he wanted to ensure Jones got the part. One of the things he wanted was to fuck Jones's boy toy of the moment. That was Gabriel.

Gabriel had been given to Martinez for the evening and night. Jay Jones had told him bluntly that he was Martinez's for the night to do whatever the man wanted to do with him—and Gabriel was to leave the man happy. Jay had come to the cottage behind his house, on the other side of the swimming pool and tennis courts, and had picked out what Gabriel was to wear—silky white jock strap and long-sleeved shirt, a tuxedo-cut ivory suit, and a red bow tie. Then Gabriel had been sent off to the Hollywood Bowl in a taxi and been told that Martinez would see that he was returned by noon the next day.

"Tell whoever he has drive you to approach through the alley and return by the back gate," Jones said. "Call me from the cottage when you're back. I'll want a full report."

71

Gabriel had retorted, "And photographs and semen samples?"

"Don't be smart," Jones had said. "You knew you would have to lay down for me and my friends in exchange for your board and keep and movie opportunities."

Gabriel knew that when Jay told him to call on the phone, he meant he wasn't to come to the main house. He only came to the main house late on a night that Jones wasn't entertaining and then the only room Gabriel saw was Jones's bedroom, which opened via a French door onto the back terrace. When Jones wanted to fuck him in the afternoon, he came to the cottage.

When the lights went down in the Hollywood Bowl, and the applause had died from Carlos Chavez's entrance and bow at the podium, and the music started, Martinez turned to Gabriel, acknowledging his presence for the first time since he sat down, put a hand on Gabriel's knee, and whispered in his ear, "You look smashing this evening, young man. We have a reception dinner to go to for Chavez afterward, during which you can mingle, and then I'll take you to bed for the night. I've looked forward to this."

None of this was a surprise to Gabriel. Jay Jones had made clear that he hadn't brought Gabriel to Los Angeles to keep him to himself. In the four months they'd been here, Gabriel had been given eye-candy extra roles in a couple of beach movies but Jones had made clear that, in exchange for being kept well, Gabriel would be what Jones called, with a laugh, his "Hollywood Ho," to be used as a party favor to further Jones's interests.

"We both knew you came to me as a prostitute," he'd said, and Gabriel couldn't gainsay that.

* * * *

72

The after-concert dinner party was more of a cocktails and assorted lumps of food standup mingle, in a ballroom of a Mexican-owned hotel near the movie studio lot in the southern quarter of Los Angeles. The party, which Julio Martinez was paying a big chunk of, and which meant he schmoozed and mingled in large gaggles of Spanish speakers far away from Gabriel, was to honor the conductor, Carlos Chavez, and assorted other Mexican personages in town. There was a smattering of movie folk from the studio, brought in by Martinez, and Gabriel knew some of these and had worked for a few who just knew him as an extra actor, used for young beefcake scenes and somehow hooked up with someone big at the studio who they weren't supposed to know about. The attention getter of the evening was Delores del Rio in person and twittering all across the room of the death earlier that month of Carmen Miranda who otherwise surely would have been here.

Initially, Gabriel became trapped speaking with these people as his Spanish was nearly nonexistent, but they invariably wanted to pump him to reveal how he had gotten invited to the party, and their guesses were coming too close, albeit falsely, to Martinez being his sugar daddy. There didn't seem to be any surprise that Martinez would be *some* young man's sugar daddy, so they seemed to have him pegged. Unfortunately, as they were quizzing Gabriel about relationships, they pretty much had him pegged as well. And speaking of pumping, more than one man followed him around with hopes of pumping him and there were women tracing him with their eyes as well, dreaming of being pumped by him.

As he knew neither Martinez nor Jones would be thrilled for it to be known that he was here to hook up with Martinez, Gabriel found himself filtering into the clutches of people who were chattering in Spanish. They didn't seem to mind that he stood at the fringe of their groups and smiled and nodded his head occasionally. He was nice eye candy for the women and for more than a few of the men, Hollywood being largely a gay, even if not acknowledged, town in the mid 1950s.

Since he couldn't talk and needed a crutch to make it seem like he was too busy with something to speak, he spent a good deal of time picking cocktail glasses and cubes of food off passing plates. It was while he was doing this that he caught the first glimpse of someone who reminded him of Adrian Ames—the young man he'd fooled around with on the sports teams in Lafayette—the young man who had gone to Lubbock and tempted Gabriel to join him there but who hadn't been there when Gabriel had final found his way to Lubbock.

The super of the apartment building in Lubbock had said that Adrian had gone to Los Angeles to break into movies. He'd made it clear, with a smirk, though, that it had been male porn movies he was breaking into.

Gabriel turned from the group he had been huddled with and pretending he was part of and walked the room, taking close looks at the waiters, in black tuxes, with serving trays. He was still looking when he felt the tug on his arm.

"So it *is* you." Gabriel recognized the voice and found himself trembling a bit as he turned and looked at Adrian. "I'd had indications you had come out to L.A. Did you hear I was out here and follow me?" The voice sounded hopeful. This wasn't the Adrian Gabriel remembered. That Adrian had been too cocky to let his voice reveal even a hint of hope like this. Nevertheless it, indeed, was Adrian Ames,

"I didn't find you in Lubbock," Gabriel said.

"I know. I heard from friends there that someone from Louisiana came looking for me. I hoped it was you. You heard I'd come out here to do movies?"

"I got into movies right there near Lubbock," Gabriel said. "Jay Jones is doing a movie at a big ranch near there. I hitched a ride out here with him in his studio's airplane. I've got some work at the studio near here. Not much. You still doing . . . porn?"

"A bit," Adrian said. "But I found I can make more money as an escort."

"So you're not a party waiter full time?"

"It's complicated. I came here as a waiter. But I'll be leaving with someone. You do what you have to do in this town. And you . . . ?"

"I'll be leaving with someone too," Gabriel answered.

"Female?"

"No, a man. A studio executive, Julio Martinez."

"So you do still swing that way?"

"Yes. I went on from where you started me."

"Ah. Well, I'd like to see you . . . I'd like . . . sometime . . "

"I think I'd like that too," Gabriel said. Oh god how he'd like that. Adrian was still a hunk. And he knew he was hung. And he was young and virile and vigorous. Jay Jones was good, but god was Gabriel ready for variety. That's why he hadn't balked at going with Julio Martinez, even though Martinez was nearly as old as Jones and had a bit of a pot belly on him.

"Do you have a place we can . . . ?" Adrian was almost apologetic. He had been so dominant with Gabriel at the time that it was almost embarrassing to see him almost grovel now.

"No, that wouldn't be possible," Gabriel said.

"You got a daddy, do you mean?" Adrian asked. "This studio guy, Martinez?"

"No. Someone else." God how he'd like to reveal that his sugar daddy was Jay Jones. But he didn't want to rub it in with Adrian. "Let's just say that I can't have anyone back to my place. And you?"

"I could figure something out. Here, I have a card. I'll write the number on the back. Don't call the number on the face of the card."

Apollo Entertainment, it said on the side opposite of the one Adrian scrawled his telephone number on. "An escort service?" Gabriel asked.

"You do what you have to do out here," Adrian answered. "You're really looking good, Gabe. If the time comes that you need . . . well, you know . . . you might try these guys."

"I'm not sure how long I'm out here for," Gabriel said. That surprised even him. He hadn't thought about it, but he had thought it was a direct turnaround flight when he'd come out here to begin with, and he'd just let himself drift into doing what others wanted. It was the submissive in him, he guessed. But now that he thought about it, he realized that he hadn't thought of it as a permanent arrangement. He still thought about Frank Doyle and Sunshine Ranch. But he had made no effort to contact Frank. Why was that, he wondered. Wasn't it embarrassment that he'd just flown away with Jay Jones? That he had just left Frank in the dust? He hadn't intended to.

And here, he was thinking about Frank when he had the man standing in front of him who he'd left Louisiana to find in the first place.

"But, yeah, I'd like to hook up with you. I'll call you soon and we'll set something up."

Adrian's answering smile was worth the plane trip to the West Coast.

* * * *

76

When it came time to leave—for Gabriel to leave, not for Julio Martinez to go—Martinez's chauffeur came into the party room and tapped Gabriel on the shoulder. They went out through the kitchens and Gabriel entered the black Cadillac limousine, with its smoked windows, and sank to the back corner of the backseat. Then he waited and waited, as the chauffeur leaned against the front fender of the limo and smoked Lucky Strikes. More than an hour later, one of the party planners leaned out of the kitchen door and signaled that Martinez was ready to go. The limousine pulled up in front of the hotel, the chauffeur opened the rear door for the studio executive, and Gabriel sank as far back into the darkness of the car's interior as he could, out of view from those on the sidewalk, until the Cadillac glided away from the curb.

Martinez fucked Gabriel in one of the VIP bungalows kept in a section in back of the administrative offices on the movie studio lot—or, rather, Gabriel rode Martinez there. The walrus-like Mexican movie executive was a lazy lover. His cock was of a nice size and he could keep it hard for an admirably long time—Gabriel was convinced that this movie people had access to some sort of erection drug that hadn't made it to the market yet—but he more or less just lay there and made Gabriel do all of the work.

He also didn't seem to be much, Gabriel thought, from the man's initial behavior, for affection or giving attention. There was some lip work and fondling in the back of the limousine, but the ride from hotel to studio lot was a short one, and Martinez didn't show any interest in cuddling when they got there. What he demonstrated he wanted was to fix himself a stiff drink at the bungalow's well-stocked bar that took up much of the living room, put a record of Latin music on that had almost given Gabriel a headache when it was played live at the Hollywood Bowl earlier and wasn't much more welcome to him now, and had Gabriel strip down to his jock strap and red bow tie and dance for him while Martinez sipped his scotch on the rocks.

Then he had Gabriel kneel in front of him, unzip him, and suck him full hard, while Martinez sang in Spanish in hushed tones to the record. Gabriel thought the man's singing was actually better than the instrumental background. A love song was being played now, though, and Gabriel managed to get turned on by a combination of the hard cock stroking inside his mouth and the Spanish being sung.

They fucked on the wide bed in the bungalow's bedroom. Martinez lay there on his back, looking a bit like a beached whale, but with a quite adequate rock-hard shaft, while Gabriel rode the cock from all four points of the compass. Jay Jones's admonition to him to make the man happy was ringing in Gabriel's ears. He retained the bow tie and the jock strap for the fuck, but Martinez did insert a hand under the pouch of the jock strap after Gabriel had ridden him facing his face, facing his feet, and now facing his left side, and masturbated Gabriel's cock to an ejaculation while Gabriel rode him.

Martinez didn't come until Gabriel had done his full circle and they were lying side by side on the bed, with Gabriel slowly jerking the heavy Mexican off and Martinez smoking a Chesterfield. Gabriel was a bit depressed, as he felt that Martinez hadn't enjoyed the fuck much. He was distant and there was no touchy feely or lip work while Gabriel was riding him.

But Gabriel was mistaken. Martinez had just been savoring the experience.

"Do you like this bungalow?" Martinez asked after he'd come and Gabriel had rolled off his side onto his back.

"Yes, it's very nice," Gabriel answered.

"It's stocked twice a week and cleaned twice a week too—on different days. That includes restocking the bar. There's a pool area on the other side of the rank of bungalow's behind this one."

"Is there?" Gabriel asked. Why was the man telling him this?

"We double up in some of the bungalows, but this one is assigned at my discretion. You could have it all to yourself."

Ah so, Gabriel thought. He liked the fuck after all. He's pitching to be my sugar daddy. "You know I live at Jay Jones's," he said.

"Now, yes, but I thought you would be looking for a new situation."

"A new situation?"

Martinez was showing more life and more interest now. He stubbed his cigarette out in an ashtray on the nightstand, turned onto his side facing Gabriel, rolled Gabriel onto his side facing away from him, and pulled the jock strap down and off Gabriel's legs.

So now he was going to do the fucking, Gabriel thought. The man was more into this than he'd previously shown.

"Jay Jones isn't known for keeping a young man for very long," Martinez murmured. "He uses the changes in his location stints to change partners. I am a steadier man, and I can be very valuable to a young man wanting to make it in the movies." Martinez's fingers were working inside Gabriel's channel.

"Yes, well, he's in the middle of filming *Big Sky Country*," Gabriel whispered, sighing for the opening attention Julio was giving him. He reached back and grasped the man's cock. He was hard as a rock. They were going to fuck again.

"We go back to Texas as soon as they've renovated the main house for the second half of the film," he added.

"The house renovations have been delayed. That's what Jay's been pestering me about. There's a movie he wanted to do with me filming down on the Baja Peninsula starting in a couple of weeks. We could do his scenes before he was needed back on the *Big Sky Country* set. And I think there's a young man in my movie he's been cultivating. I think that's why he's keen on doing this movie."

"And that's what I'm doing here?" Gabriel asked. "Being given to you to convince you to let Jay take another guy off to Mexico?"

"Do you find me repulsive?"

"No, not at all." And he didn't—at least in the dark he didn't. It all depended on the cock, and this guy's cock was more than adequate.

"Are you sensitive to Jones treating you as his property—as an asset he can give away at his own pleasure and to further his own career?"

"Yes, a little, I guess."

"I'm glad that you have some pride left. Yes, that's what Jay Jones does. He seduces young men, uses them in various ways, and discards them. I wouldn't do that to you. I'd take care of you."

Martinez was all exploring hands now, covering Gabriel's body, exploring every nook and cranny and paying attention to them. He ran the fingers of one hand into the hair on the back of Gabriel's head, turned the young man's head to him, and possessed his mouth with a demanding-tongue kiss. Gabriel gasped through the kiss as the fingers of the other hand invaded his channel and spread it open. The fingers were replaced by a hard, deep-probing cock, and the Mexican fucked Gabriel hard in a side split for several minutes and then, rolling over on top

80

of him, with Gabriel on his belly, and Martinez now saddled on him, suddenly come to life, grabbing the top of the brass headboard overhead for leverage, and pounding, pounding, pounding, as Gabriel writhed under him, his fists also gripping the brass headboard rungs for dear life, his unheeded cries for mercy transcending to cries for more, deeper, longer.

Afterward they both lay there, side by side, sweating and gasping for breath.

"So, should I hire Jay Jones for the movie down on the Baja Peninsula with you moving here?" Martinez asked. "I'll give you a car as well. A nice convertible perhaps?"

"And you'd give me the cock regularly?"

"Oh, yes, I'll give you the cock regularly. That's why I have this bungalow just steps away from my office at the studio."

~

Chapter Six: I Left My Heart in Texas

"What do you mean you are staying in New York?"

They had just had sex in the bed in one of the Roosevelt Hotel's cheaper rooms in Manhattan, convenient to Madison Square Garden, where the Rocky Marciano-Archie Moore championship prizefight would occur that evening, on September 21st, 1955. Gabe—once again Gabe, as the New York gangster he was escorting to the fight would like that better than Gabriel—had dressed and was combing his hair. He peered at Adrian Ames through the reflection in the bureau mirror. Adrian, still naked, still half hard and fondling his cock with one hand and smoking a Camel with the other after having plowed Gabe, was lying on his back, propped up on pillows, legs bent and spread, and watching Gabe finishing dressing.

They had both been brought into New York from Los Angeles by a Broadway show producer who was trying to woo a mafia don into backing his new play. Through the Apollo Entertainment escort service, Adrian had topped for the stage producer when he came to Los Angeles. When he wanted a submissive escort to match up with the New York gangster he was cultivating, Adrian had suggested Gabe.

Gabe had given the green light to Julio Martinez to give Jay Jones the part he wanted in the movie filming down on the Baja Peninsula, and Jay had then unceremoniously rousted Gabe out of his pool cottage, but that hadn't meant that Gabe had taken Martinez up on his offer to change sugar daddies. Instead, he'd tracked down Adrian, hooked up with him in bed again, and moved in with him in a studio apartment. Gabe had thought he could make it on his own as movie background fodder, but he couldn't—he'd lost the patronage of both Jay Jones and Julio Martinez. Martinez had, in fact, shown a vindictiveness toward Gabe's getting work in the studio, for Gabe having turned his offer of a kept boy toy down. Adrian had gotten him set up with Apollo Entertainment as an escort/male whore.

"But the movies. You wanted to make a try at getting into the movies," Gabe said.

"That hasn't happened. Tony says he'll get me some stage work and an Equity card. You have your Equity card; I don't. And he says he'll pay for acting lessons. In the meantime he'll hook me up with an escort service in New York that pays better than Apollo does."

"But where will you live?"

"Tony says the escort service provides the apartment—something snazzy. They go for a high-class clientele, so they give the guys and women good digs. But Tony says if I don't want to do it that way, I can live with him. He's on the hook, Gabe. He can't get enough of me. He's even going to take me with him to play openings. He's known to the queer set in New York. They think that's intellectual and chic here. He's going to acknowledge me openly. That's something no one will do in Los Angeles."

"But your apartment—our apartment—in L.A. . . . ."

"The lease is up at the end of October. I'll pay my share until then. You can keep it or get another roommate—I doubt, though, if you can find one who fucks you as good as I do." He laughed at that, but Gabe didn't join him. "You can make enough at Apollo and you've got your foot in the door in the movies."

83

Gabe didn't respond to that. He knew that the doors were being slammed on his foot in the movies. He knew that Martinez had put the word out on him. Martinez still wanted him and was using his power to get Gabe to knuckle under to him, but Gabe knew that the man would be even more possessive and dominating knowing that Gabe had resisted him and failed. Maybe if the man weren't such a big lump. And his cocking—once he got into it, he could be really rough.

"Or you could stay here," Adrian said. "You have your card and something on your résumé. You could do stage work. And you could, I'm sure, work for the same escort agency Tony will get me in with."

"And I could live with you? We could stay together?"

"We could fuck occasionally. But Tony's my meal ticket here. I'll do what Tony wants me to do. I don't think he wants me living with another guy and not being his totally eventually. You could get established on your own fast enough, though. So, what do you think?"

"What does it matter what I think, Adrian? You said this guy I'll be with tonight is a bruiser and a gangster?"

"He's probably a teddy bear," Adrian said, rolling over the edge of the bed and sitting up, ready now to prepare for the night at the fights himself. "Tony says the guy can't stop giggling that his name is Rocky and he's going to a Rocky Marciano fight."

* * * *

It was a bloody fight, and Marciano went down, in the second round, to a four count, and then, miraculously, was up again. He persisted, the two muscled warriors whaling away at each other, landing blows, dancing around, going into the clutch. Gabe thought he'd hate it, but it fascinated him. He found it sensual and arousing. The men had beautiful bodies and they almost seemed to be making love as they battered each other and went into sweaty clinches, each man fighting for dominance, trying to force the other man into submission, pounded down to the mat, with the victor standing over the panting vanquished, each bloodied and bruised, each giving his all.

They had good seats—out of the spatter of blood and sweat but close enough to see the expression on the men's faces. Both men were in a state of ecstasy. They'd both been made for this, this struggle for domination and control.

The reactions of the four men in Tony's party were very different. Tony was only here to impress Rocky. He was a submissive himself, bordering on feminine. His world was one of beauty and pretense and deception. It was the opposite of what was happening in the ring. There was a very real fight for dominance and victory in the ring. And it was raw and, in Tony's perceptions, ugly. There wasn't anything beautiful in Tony's eyes in what was going on in the ring. So he spent the fight looking down into his lap or across the audience, his eyes picking out men who he'd like to cover him.

For his part, Adrian was just bored. He saw no purpose to these two men with beautiful bodies messing each other up just for a gold metal championship belt that was too bulky to wear anywhere. They were both tops; he was a top. They were bruisers; he kept his body toned in movie star trim—waiting to become one at any moment. They were in droopy, sweat-stained shorts. He dressed to impress and had done so this evening. His mind kept going back to what he was going to have to do with Tony later that night and whether he could go hard enough to do it.

Adrian wasn't aroused by pansies. That's why he liked fucking Gabe. Gabe had a beautiful, muscular body and, though he went totally submissive, he retained the sense that he was a man. That a man would give in completely to another man like Gabe did was why men, including Adrian, liked to fuck Gabe. Tony was a pansy. And, as far as Adrian could see, he was going to have to manage to get it up for Tony for the foreseeable future. His eyes went to the ring occasionally, but his mind was skipping two years ahead. Where would he be then? What would he be doing? Who would be doing it with? Tony had asked him earlier to move his things from the Roosevelt after the fight—to go ahead and move in with him. Adrian was undecided on whether to come under Tony's sway that fast.

Rocky was in heaven. Tony had guessed perfectly in wanting to get at Rocky's interest and pocketbook. Rocky's gofer had screwed up in getting tickets to the fight, the fight of the century, as far as Rocky was concerned. Archie Moore was the world light heavyweight champion and Rocky Marciano, who had won all of his professional matches thus far, all forty-eight of them, lusted for the forty-ninth win. Rocky, cheering for Marciano simply because they had the same name, lusted for a fight to bloody subjugation, mentally putting himself in the position of a superior fighter beating down a young opponent. He lusted after men sexually too. He lusted after the young man he'd been set up with for the evening. It wasn't lost on him that Gabe was sexually aroused by the fight too. Rocky's hand went from Gabe's knee to his basket, finding the young man hard. Gabe's gaze at the ring was hard too, his eyes glittering. Rocky could hardly wait to get Gabe alone in the hotel suite Tony had booked for them near Madison Square Garden.

Rocky Marciano knocked Archie Moore out in the ninth round, winning the forty-ninth of his forty-nine professional fights—and retired before fighting in the professional ring again.

The two couples split at the end of the fight, Rocky so anxious to get Gabe to the suite Tony had gotten him at the Hotel Pennsylvania at Seventh Avenue and 33rd Street that he barely acknowledged Tony and Adrian when they left. Gabe was so keyed up for sex that he went with the all-hands hustle the short distance to the hotel and up to the suite.

Once in the suite, the fuck became very different to any Gabe had had before. The two men went into a standing clutch just inside the door, tearing at each other's clothes, their mouths in a lip lock and their hands exploring and grabbing. Gabe almost hyperventilated when he discovered that Rocky was carrying—that he had a shoulder holster under his suit coat and a nasty-looking hand gun. That became a worry for later, though, when, basically stripped down except for the holster, with its chest harness, on Rocky's bare, meaty, and heavily hirsute chest, Rocky punched Gabe in the gut and then caught him on the chin with an upper cut to the jaw.

Gabe put up a fight of it—he wasn't a pushover—but Rocky had him by surprise, an initial getting ahead of the count, and a good fifty pounds. Keyed up by the prize fight they'd just seen and full of blood lust, Rocky pounded Gabe into submission. Gabe went to the mat in round one.

Rocky fucked him on the floor, covering him doggie style and ramming him hard. Gabe blacked out and when he came to, he was stretched out on the bed, his wrists bound by his leather belt and hooked on a decorative spike on the headboard. Rocky was fucking him in a missionary, and, seeing that Gabe was awake, he rammed the barrel of his gun under Gabe's chin and told him to take it. He continued to fuck him hard and Gabe took it. He almost tossed his dinner when he heard the click of the gun and

Rocky's laugh. And then he passed out again while Rocky was choking him.

The next time he woke, he was in the hospital. He was told that he was found, thankfully with his trousers on, on the floor of an elevator when it opened in the hotel lobby. A policeman visited him in the hospital, but Gabe claimed to be hazy about anything that had happened after he'd left his room at the Roosevelt to check out Times Square. He had no illusions about how he would fare if he made any mention of Rocky and the mafia or led the police to Tony. Neither Adrian nor Tony showed up at the hospital.

He was in the hospital for three days. When he got out, he went to the Roosevelt, to be told that Adrian had checked out three days earlier and the hotel bill had been paid. They had kept Gabe's suitcase with the clothes he'd brought to New York in their holding room.

Gabe went from the hotel to the airport. He made a phone call and then turned in his return-flight ticket to Los Angeles, buying a ticket to another destination altogether.

* * * *

"God, Gabe, you look like you were run over by a dump truck. You OK?"

"Thanks for asking, Frank. So, you're not glad to see me unless I'm tied up in a pretty bow." Gabe was aware that Frank Doyle had been hopping up and down like a puppy dog and raced down from the observation deck of the Lubbock, Texas, airport to the baggage claim area the moment Gabe had climbed out of the plane.

"Of course I'm glad to see you. I'm been pissing myself with anxiety to see you ever since you called me from New York. Were you mugged there, or what? And I thought you had gone to Los Angeles—with Jay Jones. But about Jay Jones—"

"Yes, I'm OK, Frank. Good to see you too. I can carry my own bag, thanks. And thanks for coming into Lubbock to pick me up."

"I would have gone to New York to pick you up, Gabe. But about Jay Jones. I assume you've flown in because you heard he came back to finish off that movie being filmed at Brighton Ranch. But you should know—"

"No I didn't come here for Jones, Frank," Gabe said. "A lot has happened since I was with Jay Jones. And that's a story best not picked apart."

"I'm glad to hear that," Frank answered. And, indeed, he looked very relieved. "Because I'm afraid Jones is dead. He roared out in the yellow Ford Sunliner we saw over there when you went to work there, and damned if he didn't wrap that around the same telephone pole that other actor, Collin Chisholm, hit with his motorcycle."

Gabe dropped his suitcase and stood still in his tracks. They were half way between the terminal doors and the parking lot. "Look at me Frank. I'm sorry Jay Jones is dead. But my thing with Jay Jones died some time ago. All of my fancy plans for what I thought I wanted to do with my life died a couple of nights ago. Jones was just a user. Nearly all of the men I've been with were just users—all but one. I had reality beat into me and I had time lying in a hospital bed to think about what I really wanted. What I really want, Frank, is you . . . and a life at Sunshine Ranch with you. If I haven't burnt my bridges with you. I know I treated you rotten. I know—"

"Shut up and get in the car, Gabe," Frank said, his voice choked up. "I can't wait to get you to the ranch. I can't wait to get you home."

"And into bed?"

"Well, we have a couple of new horses to break in, and you're the best one I've known to be able to do that."

"Oh," Gabe answered.

"Well, and, yes, to get you into bed."

Both men grinned.

~

About the Author

An artist and writer, Dirk has always been interested in history and legends, particularly those of the United States, the Mediterranean, and Asia. His works are historical, and sometimes border on fantasy. They are full of ordinary men struggling to survive and find love in difficult situations. And sometimes Dirk writes about men who are in touch with forces beyond those of mortal men, fighting for survival in more unusual ways.

Dirk's books often, but not always, contain male sex that is both forceful and rough, and at times dangerous, but is always within the context of stories of survival in more primitive and brutal times. He also writes about the power of love in turbulent times.

He can be found at the adults only gay male site BarbarianSpy, which he shares with Sabb and habu (sr71plt).

You can send feedback about this ebook directly to Dirk, or send general feedback on this ebook to BarbarianSpy.

Our authors always like to receive feedback, and appreciate it when readers post reviews at distributors and review sites.

BarbarianSpy

FOR LITERARY HEAT

BarbarianSpy Books

Not all books listed below may currently be on release.
* indicates the book is available in paperback and e-book.

BOOKS BY CHRIS CROSS
Multisexual Adult Romance

Pulaski Square
Chocolate in Vanilla (MF)2
Christmas with Chris (MMF) (MM) (MF)

BOOKS BY ALEX LOCKHEED
Transgender Romance

Meeting Jenna

Transgender Other

Being Sarah

BOOKS BY DIRK HESSIAN
Xtreme Historical Erotica

Dirk's Ancient Times Collection (Print only Bundle)*
The King's Men
Shores of Tripoli*
Prophecy of Noto
Pretender's Fate

General Historical Erotic Romance

Dirk's America's Founding Collection (Print only Bundle)*
Soldier,Spy
Ridden West
Deliver a Virgin
Clouds and Rain
Confederate Gold
Puttin on the Ritz
To the Hessian Hills
Fire Down the Valley*
Constantinople*
The Beautiful Way*
Blue and Gray
Colonel's Treasure
Beginning of Time
Labyrinth

BOOKS BY HABU
Gay Erotica
Memoir Faction
Flying High, Diving Deep*
Xtreme Erotica
Fist of Gold
Liaisons
Chain Gang Banged (Short Story)
Tramp Steaming*
Escape to Girne
Silas' Choice*
Last Call
Choke Hold
Apyko: The Greek Pimp
Visits of the Schlange
Second Coming: Emile La Cour Unleashed*
Vortex: Sacrificed by Curiosity*
Dark Angel Sounding *(in e-book & included in Sounding:Ultimate Control paperback)*
Sounding: Ultimate Control (*Print Only*)*
Sounding Five *(in e-book & included in Sounding:Ultimate Control paperback)*
Romance
Gift from the Sea
Shore Leave
The Aviators
Poison Pen
Need to be Needed
Key Westing (short)
Finding a New Sam
Bangkok Summer Seduction
The Photograph
Inevitable Case
Turn to Love
Rain Check
Built for Pleasure (Sci Fi)
Danny's Choice*
Pull of the Groove
Sugar n Spice Christmas
Friday Nights with Lenny (Christmas Romance)
Snowy, Snowy Nights (Christmas Romance)
Tank n Bull
Sail to the Sun

War Letters
Ravens Roost
Caribbean Cruise Top to Bottom
Arena Stage
Trading Partners (Valentine's Day)
Four Coins
Lower Than the Heart (Valentine's Day)
Brambleton
Finding Amnad
Platres Conclave

Other Novels/Novellas

Also Want to Thank
Ranger Guided
Key Westing
Syrian Ram
Temptation's Clutches*
Descent into Chaos
Escape to Girne
Journey Through Abilene
Harmony and Dissonance
Stallion Station
Racing With the Devil (espionage suspense)
Prepared in Cape Verdi
Gilded Cage
House on Park*
Anything for Ambition
Dance of the Ravishers
Hard Knocks U*
My Neighbor's Spa*
Man's Man: Tales of a High Priced Gay Hooker*
Trip Money
The Indian Doctor
Sailorboy
Home to Fire Island
Switching Sides*

Murder Mysteries

Retribution (Hardesty)
Snitches (Hardesty
Gotta Keep Trying (Hardesty)
All Fools Day Foolery (Mike Kavanagh)
Inevitable Case (Mike Kavanagh)
Vanishing Laura
Death on a Ping Pong Table
Clint Folsom Mysteries Compendium Volume 1*
Death to Blonds - Stolen Judgment (Clint Folsom Mystery)*

94

Clint Folsom Mysteries Compendium Volume 2*

Gay Erotica Anthologies

A Hell of a War*

Earth Cry*

Shunga

Habu's Christmas Balls

Eight in D*

DevilMENt

Silas' Choices*

Stallion Station (A Novella in Parts)

Eleven to the Dogs*

Fifty Seventy*

Spy Tails 001*

Spy Tails 002*

Doubled*

Doubled Again*

Tails in the Tropics*

Tails in the Med*

Tails in the West*

Rough Riders*

Grab Bag 1*

Grab Bag 2*

Grab Bag 3*

Grab Bag 4*

Grab Bag 5*

Grab Bag 6*

Grab Bag 7*

Grab Bag 8*

Grab Bag 9*

Grab Bag 10*

Grab Bag 11*

Grab Bag 12

Grab Bag 13*

Beyond the Beaded Curtain*

The Sporting Life*

Fetish Galore!*

Literary Gay Erotica

Cairo Surrender*

The Handyman*

Homeward Bound

Journey to Mirage*

Bisexual/Menage/Multisexual Erotica

And Eat it Too

Two Men, One Woman*

Every Which Way

95

Summer of Denial
Death on a Ping Pong Table
Cruising Gigolo
13 Ways for Halloween
Luther*
The Indian Prince*
BOOKS BY SABB
Spanish Lovers
Driver Reliever
Hiring in Hollywood
The Legend of Holleystone Grange
Surprise Encounters*
She is He
Wrong Man
Loyal to his King
Barbarian Tales - Book One - Traveler's Tales*
Barbarian Tales - Book Two - Journeys Begin*
Barbarian Tales - Book Three - The Inheritance*
Barbarian Tales - Book Four - Road to Persepolis*
BOOKS BY SHABBU
A Season in Galicia*
Blind Dates*
Velvet Interrogation
Finding Jason
Dirty Pool
Operation Black Jade
Cigars!*
Angel in the Barn
Gayly Complicated*
Despoiling David
The Tree of Idleness*
I Met a Man
Rough Road to Happiness
BOOKS BY STEPHEN KESSEL
Gay Romance
The Forever Man
Two Chances
BOOKS BY KIM BLACK
Lesbian Romance
Transfixed on Tammie (F/T lesbian)

~

www.ingramcontent.com/pod-product-compliance
Lightning Source LLC
Chambersburg PA
CBHW020631130626
46552CB00003B/1178